# KINGDOM BY THE SEA

## *Edgar Allan Poe's Charleston Tales*

*Edited by Mark R. Jones*

## ALSO BY MARK R. JONES

*Doin' the Charleston: Black Roots of American Popular Music & the Jenkins Orphanage Legacy* (2013)

*South Carolina Killers: Crimes of Passion* (2007)

*Palmetto Predators: Monsters Among Us* (2007)

*Wicked Charleston, Vol II: Prostitutes, Politics & Prohibition* (2006)

*Wicked Charleston: The Dark Side of the Holy City* (2005)

# KINGDOM BY THE SEA

## Edgar Allan Poe's Charleston Tales

Edited by Mark R. Jones

Introduction and notes by Mark R. Jones.

Copyright © 2013

All Rights Reserved. No part of this book may be reproduced or transmitted in any form or by any means, electronic or mechanical, including photocopying, recording, or by any information storage and retrieval system – except by a reviewer who may quote brief passages in a review to be printed in a magazine, newspaper, or on the Web – without permission in writing from the publisher. Please contact:

East Atlantic Publishing: 1323 Jackwood Court, Charleston, SC, 29407.
**editor@eastatlanticpublishing.com**

Although the editor and publisher have made every effort to ensure the accuracy and completeness of information contained in this book, we assume no responsibility for errors, inaccuracies, omissions or any inconsistency herein.

"The Gold Bug" originally published in the *Philadelphia Dollar Newspaper,* 1843.

"The Oblong Box" originally published in *Godey's Magazine and Lady's Book,* 1844.

"The Balloon-Hoax" originally published in *The Sun,* New York City, 1844.

"Annabel Lee" originally published in the New York *Daily Tribune*, October 9, 1849, two days after Poe's death as part of his obituary.

First Edition

First Printing 2013

ISBN-13: 978-0615886664
ISBN-10: 0615886663

Printed in the United States of America

# TABLE OF CONTENTS

**Edgar Allan Poe. Daguerreotype by W.S. Hartshorn, 1848.**
***Courtesy of the Library of Congress***

# Edgar Allan Poe Timeline

## 1809

••••••••••••••••••••••••••••••••••••••••••••••••••••

**January 19th**: Edgar Allan Poe is born in Boston, Massachusetts. Poe's parents were actors, David and Eliza Arnold Hopkins Poe. Eliza, born in England, is a well-known ingénue and comedienne.

## 1810

••••••••••••••••••••••••••••••••••••••••••••••••••••

When Poe is two-years old, his father abandons the family. For the next year Mrs. Poe, although in ill health, continues to appear in various acting roles in Norfolk, Va., Charleston, S. C. and Richmond.

## 1811

••••••••••••••••••••••••••••••••••••••••••••••••••••

**December 8th**. Poe's mother, Eliza, is overtaken by illness and dies in Richmond. Two days later she is buried in the churchyard of St. John's Episcopal Church. Edgar and his sister, Rosalie, are placed in the care of a wealthy English merchant, John Allan, and his wife, Frances from Richmond. His brother, Henry, is placed with another family.

## 1815

••••••••••••••••••••••••••••••••••••••••••••••••••

The Allans, who never officially adopt the two children, move to England for an extended business trip. Though frugal, John Allen recognizes the importance of a good education. Edgar shows an early gift for language and receives the best education while in England, spending time at prestigious boarding academies in London and in suburban Stoke-Newington.

## 1820

••••••••••••••••••••••••••••••••••••••••••••••••••

The Allans return to Richmond and Edgar resumes schooling in private academies, showing aptitude for Latin, acting, swimming, and poetry.

## 1824

••••••••••••••••••••••••••••••••••••••••••••••••••

Poe, age 15, serves as the lieutenant of the Richmond Youth Honor Guard, celebrating the visit of the Marquis de Lafayette.

## 1825

••••••••••••••••••••••••••••••••••••••••••••••••••

John Allan's uncle and business benefactor William Galt dies and leaves Allan an inheritance estimated at $750,000. Allan purchases a two-story brick home named Moldavia.

Poe becomes engaged to Sarah Elmira Royster, a neighbor friend he has known since childhood. Sarah's parents, however, are not enthused about the engagement.

### *1826* ........................................

Poe attends the University of Virginia and distinguishes himself in ancient and modern languages. While in school Poe loses touch with Sarah Royster. His letters to her are never answered so he stops writing.

Allan provides Poe with one-third of the money needed for the school year. Living the life of a Virginia gentleman Poe begins to gamble to raise money and is soon in debt by $2,000. The university, established by Thomas Jefferson, has strict rules against gambling, horses, guns, tobacco and alcohol, but these rules are generally ignored.

Allan refuses to pay his gambling debts, regarding them as a young man's "debts of honor." John Allan hopes that Poe will join his own mercantile firm, but Poe is determined to become a writer and, in particular, a poet.

Without money, Poe returns briefly to Richmond. He discovers that under the direction of her family, his fiancée Sarah Elmira Royster, has married an older and wealthier suitor, Alexander Shelton.

Poe and Allan quarrel constantly over the young man's future.

## 1827

••••••••••••••••••••••••••••••••••••••••••••••••••••

Poe moves to Boston, Massachusetts, supporting himself with odd jobs as a clerk and newspaper writer. Poverty forces him to join the U.S. Army. He enlists under the assumed name, Edgar Perry, claiming to be 22-years old even though he is only 18. During his military training, he writes romantic poetry in the tradition of Lord Byron. His first volume of poems was published in 1827 as *Tamerlane and Other Poems*, "By a Bostonian." Only 50 copies were printed, and the book received virtually no attention.

**November 8:** Poe's regiment is posted to Fort Moultrie in Charleston, South Carolina. Poe is promoted to "artificer," an enlisted tradesman who prepared shells for artillery. His monthly pay doubled.

## 1829

••••••••••••••••••••••••••••••••••••••••••••••••••••

After two years Poe attains the rank of Sergeant Major for Artillery, the highest rank a non-commissioned officer can achieve. He seeks to end his five-year enlistment early. He reveals his real name and his circumstances to his commanding officer, Lieutenant Howard. Howard agrees to allow the discharge if Poe reconciles with John Allan.

Several months pass and Poe's pleas to Allan are ignored. Poe's foster mother, Frances Allan, dies in Richmond.

Poe wins his release by providing a substitute for his military enrollment. Poe applies to West Point, and moves to Baltimore to live with his widowed aunt, Maria Clemm, her daughter, Virginia Eliza Clemm (Poe's first cousin), his brother Henry, and his invalid grandmother Elizabeth Cairnes Poe. His second book, *Al Aaraaf, Tamerlane and Minor Poems,* is published in Baltimore. Most of these poems were written while stationed at Ft. Moultrie.

## 1830

**July 1:** Enrolls at West Point.

**October:** John Allan marries his second wife, Louisa Patterson. Poe and Allan have bitter quarrels over Allan's illegitimate children born due to his many affairs. Allan disowns Poe.

## 1831

Poe decides to leave West Point. He purposely gets himself court-martialed for gross neglect of duty and disobedience of orders for refusing to attend formations, classes, or church.

**February:** A third volume of poems, simply titled *Poems,* is published. The book is financed with help from his fellow cadets at West Point, many of whom donated 75 cents to the cause, raising a total of $170.

**March:** Returns to Baltimore, living with his aunt, brother and cousin.

**August:** Poe's brother, Henry, dies of tuberculosis.

## 1833

Edgar Allan Poe wins $50 from the *Baltimore Saturday Visitor* for his short story, "MS Found in a Bottle." His "The Coliseum" places second for poetry. Both appear in *Visitor* in October 1833. He continues to live in the Baltimore home of his paternal grandmother with his Aunt Maria Clemm and her children, Virginia and Henry.

## 1834

Poe's tale "The Visionary" appears in January 1834 issue of *Godey's Lady's Book*, a national publication. John Allan dies in March 1834 and leaves Poe nothing.

## 1835

Poe begins contributing to Richmond's *Southern Literary Messenger*, including "The Unparalleled Adventure of One Hans Pfaall," considered the first modern science fiction story. Moves to Richmond, joins the *Messenger* staff and dramatically increases the magazine's circulation and national reputation.

He returns to Baltimore and begins to court his cousin Virginia. Returns to Richmond with Mrs. Clemm and Virginia and files for marriage license in Baltimore to marry his cousin, Virginia Clemm.

Hired as the *Messenger's* new editor, Poe writes book reviews, stories, and poems.

## 1836

Poe and Virginia are married by a Presbyterian minister, Rev. Amasa Converse. Poe is 27 and Virginia 13, though her age is listed as 21.

## 1837

Resigns from *Messenger*, partly due to his alcoholism. Takes family to New York to seek employment but is unable to find editorial post.

## 1838

Publishes poems and tales, including "Ligeia." Mrs. Clemm manages a boarding house to help make ends meet.

**July.** *Harper's* publishes *The Narrative of Arthur Gordon Pym,* Poe's only completed novel. Moves family to Philadelphia and continues to freelance but considers giving up literary work.

## 1839

Works as editor for *Burton's Gentleman's Magazine* in Philadelphia. Poe agrees to provide eleven pages of original material per month and is paid $10 a week. During that year Poe publishes "The Man That Was Used Up," "The Fall of the House of Usher," "William Wilson," and "Morella."

In severe financial straits, Poe agrees to let name appear as author of a cut-price naturalists' manual, *The Conchologist's First Book.*

## 1841

Poe's first book of short stories, *Tales of the Grotesque and Arabesque,* is published, dedicated to Colonel William Drayton of South Carolina whom Poe met while stationed in Charleston. Drayton was part of the South Carolina low country planter class, a former member of Congress and may have subsidized the book's publication.

Frustrated with his lack of financial success, Poe becomes a champion for the cause of higher wages for writers and lobbies for an international copyright law.

Poe is dismissed from *Burton's Gentleman's Magazine* for arguing with the owner. George Rex Graham, former editor of the *Saturday Evening Post* purchases *Burton's* and creates *Graham's Magazine*, to which Poe contributes "The Man of the Crowd."

Becomes editor of *Graham's Magazine* in Philadelphia. Poe contributes "The Murders in the Rue Morgue," the first modern detective story. He also writes poems, and articles on cryptography. Under Graham's direction Poe begins to publish the harsh critical literary reviews for which he becomes famous. By year's end, *Graham's* subscriptions go from 5000 to 25,000.

## 1842

**January:** Virginia bursts a blood vessel while singing and playing the piano. She exhibits signs of tuberculosis. Poe begins to drink more heavily under the stress of Virginia's illness.

Poe meets Charles Dickens and publishes "The Masque of the Red Death," "The Pit and the Pendulum" and the literary-defining review of Hawthorne's *Twice Told Tales.*

He leaves *Graham's* to return to New York, and works briefly at the *Evening Mirror* before becoming editor of the *Broadway Journal.*

## 1843

Contributes "The Tell-Tale Heart," "Lenore," and an essay later titled "The Rationale of Verse" to James Russell Lowell's magazine *The Pioneer.*

Goes to Washington D.C. to be interviewed for minor post in Tyler administration and to solicit subscriptions for his own journal, *The Stylus*; gets drunk and ruins his chances for the government job. Resumes writing satires, poems and reviews but is pressed to borrow money from friends.

"The Gold Bug" wins $100 prize in newspaper contest and is reprinted widely, then dramatized on the Philadelphia stage, making Poe famous as a popular writer. A pamphlet titled *The Prose Romances of Edgar A. Poe,* appears in July and includes "The Murders in the Rue Morgue."

Poe enters the lecture circuit, presenting a speech titled "The Poets and Poetry of America." Publishes "The Pit and the Pendulum," "The Tell-Tale Heart," and "The Black Cat."

## 1844

Writes "The Oblong Box" and "The Premature Burial" and a "news story" in the *New York Sun* about a successful trans-Atlantic balloon flight from Europe to Charleston. The story creates a national sensation until Poe reveals the entire episode was made up.

## 1845

"The Raven" appears in the *January Evening Mirror* and creates a national sensation. Poe becomes a national figure and enters New York literary society.

Putnam publishes *Poe's Tales,* then *The Raven and Other Poems.*

Poe borrows money to acquire controlling interest in *The Broadway Journal.*

He conducts literary courtship in verse with poet Frances Sargent Osgood and initiates the "Little

Longfellow War," a private campaign against plagiarism, with Henry Wordsworth Longfellow as the most eminent of those accused. The campaign brings more notoriety but alienates Poe's literary friends. Negative publicity from his reading at the *Boston Lyceum*, and the insulting jibes against Boston with which Poe responds, further damage his reputation but increases his fame.

Virginia's illness becomes acute.

## 1846

Illness, nervous depression, and hardship force Poe to stop publication of *The Broadway Journal*. Moves his family to a cottage in Fordham, New York, where Virginia, now an invalid, is nursed by family friend Marie Louise Shew. Poe and his family are mentioned in the New York press as pitiable charity cases.

Poe manages to publish "The Cask of Amontillado," "The Philosophy of Composition," book reviews, and "Marginalia" in various magazines.

He also begins a series of satirical sketches of "The Literati of New York City" in *Godey's*. The one on Thomas Dunn English, whom Poe had known in Philadelphia, draws a vicious attack by English on Poe's morality and sanity. Poe sues *The Evening Mirror*, publisher of the piece, and collects damages the following year.

## 1847

January 30. Virginia Poe dies of tuberculosis. Poe himself falls gravely ill and is nursed back to health by Mrs. Clemm and Mrs. Shew.

## 1848

Poe's health recovers. He gives lectures and readings to raise capital for the opening of *The Stylus.*

While lecturing in Lowell, Massachusetts, Poe forms deep attachment to "Annie" (Mrs. Nancy Richmond), who becomes his confidante.

In Providence, Rhode Island, Poe begins a three-month courtship of widowed poet Sarah Helen Whitman, to whom he proposes marriage. She delays answering him because of reports of his "unprincipled" character. Poe becomes angry and their brief engagement is broken off.

Reads "The Poetic Principle" as lecture to an audience of 1,800 in Providence." Writes "The Bells."

## 1849

Active as writer and lecturer. Stops in Philadelphia, sick, confused and apparently suffering from persecution mania. Friends care for him and see him off to Richmond. Recovers during two-month stay in Richmond, visits his sister Rosalie and joins the temperance society.

While in Richmond, he learns his first fiancée, Elmira Royston Shelton, is now a widow. They resume their relationship after they discover that their letters to each other while he was in college had been intercepted by Elmira's parents.

Writes "Annabel Lee."

Poe leaves for Baltimore, intending to bring Mrs. Clemm to Richmond from New York.

**October 3.** Poe is found on the streets of Baltimore delirious, "in great distress, and ... in need of immediate assistance," according to the man who found him, Joseph W. Walker.

Poe is taken to Washington College Hospital, but is never coherent long enough to explain how he came to be in his condition. More strangely, he is wearing clothes that are not his own. Poe repeatedly calls out the name "Reynolds" on the night before his death.

**Sunday, October 7**. Poe dies at 5:00 in the morning. Newspapers at the time reported Poe's death as "congestion of the brain" or "cerebral inflammation," common euphemisms for deaths from disreputable causes such as alcoholism. The actual cause of death remains a mystery; speculation has included delirium tremens, heart disease, epilepsy, syphilis, meningeal inflammation, cholera or rabies.

"Annabel Lee" is published as part of Poe's obituary.

**Edgar Allan Poe, by William Sartain, New York.**
***Courtesy of the Library of Congress***

# Introduction

EDGAR ALLAN POE IS OFTEN CALLED THE MASTER of macabre but a more fitting description is "master of melancholy." Almost every Poe tale and poem is infused with a brooding sense of overwhelming despondency. The horror in a Poe tale is more often a tortured soul rather than a tortured body. And there is no American city with a more tortured soul and profound sense of melancholy than Charleston, South Carolina.

Charles Town (as it was originally called), was founded in 1670, and quickly became one the richest and most important cities in Colonial America. Often called "Little London," it was the most cosmopolitan city in the New World, reflecting the ideals of the English aristocracy. The port was described by Governor James Glen as "a kind of floating market" in 1751. Edward McCrady wrote that, "Merchandise and trade were the foundation stones of most, if not all, the great fortunes in South Carolina." Deerskins, beaver pelts, lumber, pitch, turpentine rice, tobacco, cotton and indigo were traded for rum, sugar, land and Negro slaves.

The Charleston merchants of the early 1700s were not aristocrats; they were English, Irish, Scottish, French, German and Barbadian middle-class traders and farmers who built their fortunes through hard work. As their wealth increased, they brought huge tracts of land and became great planters of rice, indigo and tobacco. They also began to formulate their own aristocratic society, based on the ideal of the English country gentleman. Their sons and daughters were sent back to Europe for education and refinement. By the time of the American Revolution, Charleston had embraced the mantel of "little London."

The opening credits of the epic film *Gone With The Wind* accurately describes 19th century Charleston (with much romantic hindsight):

> There was a land of Cavaliers and Cotton Fields called the Old South. Here in this pretty world, Gallantry took its last bow. Here was the last ever to be seen of Knights and their Ladies Fair, of Master and of Slave.

In 1827 Charleston was a city of exquisite manners and opulence, but also a city of African pagan ritual and superstition. The city's population of 18,924 included more than 10,000 blacks, making whites a minority. This created a delicate social ballet to balance the two opposing cultures. Historians agree that at least 40% of enslaved Africans brought to America entered through Charleston. The history of the city cannot be told without delving into the culture, folklore, root magic and superstitions of the African "Gullah" population.

**Charleston, S.C., Meeting Street, circa 1850.**
***Courtesy of the Library of Congress***

The majority of Africans imported into South Carolina were from Sierra Leone and Ghana. Valued by the whites for their skills in rice cultivation these Africans placed an equal value on their own cultural heritage, which they managed to establish along the Carolina and Georgia coastal Sea Islands. Outside of Charleston, away from the mansions, gardens and towering church steeples, the landscape of the Carolina Lowcountry was a foreboding collection of swamps, salt marshes and creeks, filled with exotic and dangerous creatures. At night, the sound of African drums and singing-shouting could often be heard echoing across miles of wilderness, mixed with the bellow of gators, the howl of wolves and the roar of panthers and bobcats.

It was to this Charleston that Edgar Allan Poe arrived in November 1827. In order to escape gambling debts, poverty and a combative relationship with his adopted father, Poe enlisted in the U.S. Army under the name "Edgar Perry." Private Perry arrived on the brig *Waltham* and spent fourteen months in the South Carolina Lowcountry stationed at Ft. Moultrie on Sullivan's Island.

Poe's military duties gave him ample time for writing and exploring the wild, exotic landscape of Sullivan's Island. The description of the island in "The Gold Bug" is a very accurate one. It was a desolate place of myrtle bushes, palmetto and magnolia trees, thick underbrush and sand hills, filled with wildlife – bugs, spiders, reptiles, rabbits and rats. It is easy to see how this desolate place would have made an impression on Poe, a man of brooding melancholy and romantic sensibility.

It has long been speculated that during Poe's explorations he met Dr. Edmund Ravenel, a professor at the Medical College of South Carolina. Although Ravenel lived in his father-in-law's fashionable mansion in Charleston (54 Meeting Street) he also owned a cottage on the island. He spent years exploring Sullivan's

Island gathering a comprehensive collection of local sea shells becoming one of America's foremost conchologists. His shell collection is now housed in the Charleston Museum. It is easy to see how Poe's relationship with Dr. Ravenel could have inspired "The Gold Bug."

**Ft. Moultrie, Charleston harbor, circa 1865.**
***Courtesy of the Library of Congress.***

Charleston legend also stipulates that while stationed at Ft. Moultrie one night in a tavern Poe heard the tragic story of a local young aristocratic maiden. Her father refused the marriage proposal of a young soldier stationed in Charleston due to his lack of social status. The girl lost the will to live, becoming a shell of herself, and began to waste away. Due to her infirm condition she soon contracted an illness and died.

Poe's work is filled with tragic heroines who die at a young age, and characters who suffer unrequited love. Poe's first love was denied him while he was away at college, and he later watched his young wife suffer and waste away before him.

The contrasting Lowcountry atmosphere of sparkling gallantry, dreadful human bondage, pagan superstition and lush tropical climate fed Poe's brooding personality and inspired his dark creativity. As these four following tales indicate, Charleston insinuated herself into Poe's soul and helped spark one of the American literary geniuses of the 19th century.

# The Gold Bug

## *1843*

"The Gold Bug" illustration by "Herpin" for the 1895 *The Tales and Poems,* published in Philadelphia by George Barrie. *Courtesy of the Library of Congresss*

**"It will be found, in fact, that the ingenious are always fanciful, and the truly imaginative never otherwise than analytic."**

**-- Edgar Allan Poe**

---

Poe originally sold "The Gold-Bug" to George Rex Graham for *Graham's Magazine* for $52. However, after hearing about a writing contest sponsored by Philadelphia's *Dollar Newspaper*, Poe asked for it back so he could submit it. The story won the grand prize, $100 and was published in the newspaper in two installments on June 21 and June 28, 1843. The $100 payment was the most Poe was ever paid for a single work.

Further re-printings in United States newspapers made "The Gold-Bug" Poe's most widely read short story during his lifetime. By May 1844, Poe reported that it had circulated 300,000 copies, though he was probably not paid for these reprints. It helped increase his popularity as a lecturer and popularized cryptograms and secret writing.

William F. Friedman, America's foremost cryptologist, initially became interested in cryptography after reading "The Gold-Bug" as a child. During World War I Friedman became the personal cryptographer for General and in 1921 he became chief cryptanalyst for the War Department. "The Gold-Bug"" also includes the first use of the term "cryptograph" (as opposed to "cryptogram".)

"The Gold-Bug" also inspired Robert Louis Stevenson to write his novel, *Treasure Island* (1883). Stevenson acknowledged this influence: "I broke into the gallery of Mr. Poe ... No doubt the skeleton [in my novel] is conveyed from Poe."

Poe's depiction of the freed African slave Jupiter is racist and stereotypical from our modern perspective. Jupiter is superstitious and so lacking in intelligence that he cannot tell his left from his right. Black characters in fiction during this time period were not unusual, but Poe's choice to give Jupiter a major speaking role was. Critics and scholars have questioned if Jupiter's accent was authentic or merely comic relief. Anyone familiar with the Gullah culture of the South Carolina Lowcountry will recognize Poe's use of their familiar cadence and dialect.

# THE GOLD BUG

What ho! what ho! this fellow is dancing mad!
He hath been bitten by the Tarantula.
--All in the Wrong.

---

MANY YEARS AGO, I CONTRACTED AN INTIMACY WITH a Mr. William Legrand. He was of an ancient Huguenot family, and had once been wealthy: but a series of misfortunes had reduced him to want. To avoid the mortification consequent upon his disasters, he left New Orleans, the city of his forefathers, and took up his residence at Sullivan's Island, near Charleston, South Carolina.

This island is a very singular one. It consists of little else than the sea sand, and is about three miles long. Its breadth at no point exceeds a quarter of a mile. It is separated from the mainland by a scarcely perceptible creek, oozing its way through a wilderness of reeds and slime, a favorite resort of the marsh hen. The vegetation, as might be supposed, is scant, or at least dwarfish. No trees of any magnitude are to be seen. Near the western extremity, where Fort Moultrie stands, and where are some miserable frame buildings, tenanted, during summer, by the fugitives from Charleston dust and fever, may be found, indeed, the bristly palmetto; but the whole island, with the exception of this western point, and a line of hard, white beach on the seacoast, is covered with a dense undergrowth of the sweet myrtle so much prized by the horticulturists of England. The shrub here often attains the height of fifteen or twenty feet, and forms an almost impenetrable coppice, burdening the air with its fragrance.

In the inmost recesses of this coppice, not far from the eastern or more remote end of the island, Legrand had built himself a small hut, which he occupied when I first, by mere accident, made his acquaintance. This soon ripened into friendship--for there was much in the recluse to excite interest and esteem. I found him well educated, with unusual powers of mind, but infected with misanthropy, and subject to perverse moods of alternate enthusiasm and melancholy. He had with him many books, but rarely employed them. His chief amusements were gunning and fishing, or sauntering along the beach and through the myrtles, in quest of shells or entomological specimens--his collection of the latter might have been envied by a Swammerdamm. In these excursions he was usually accompanied by an old negro, called Jupiter, who had been manumitted before the reverses of the family, but who could be induced, neither by threats nor by promises, to abandon what he considered his right of attendance upon the footsteps of his young "Massa Will." It is not improbable that the relatives of Legrand, conceiving him to be somewhat unsettled in intellect, had contrived to instill this obstinacy into Jupiter, with a view to the supervision and guardianship of the wanderer.

The winters in the latitude of Sullivan's Island are seldom very severe, and in the fall of the year it is a rare event indeed when a fire is considered necessary. About the middle of October, 18--, there occurred, however, a day of remarkable chilliness. Just before sunset I scrambled my way through the evergreens to the hut of my friend, whom I had not visited for several weeks--my residence being, at that time, in Charleston, a distance of nine miles from the island, while the facilities of passage and repassage were very far behind those of the present day. Upon reaching the hut I rapped, as was my custom, and getting no reply, sought for the key where I knew it was secreted, unlocked the door, and went in. A fine fire was blazing upon the hearth. It was a novelty, and by no means an ungrateful one. I threw off an overcoat, took an armchair by the crackling logs, and awaited patiently the arrival of my hosts.

Soon after dark they arrived, and gave me a most cordial welcome. Jupiter, grinning from ear to ear, bustled about to prepare some marsh hens for supper. Legrand was in one of his fits--how else shall I term them?--of enthusiasm. He had found an unknown bivalve, forming a new genus, and, more than this, he had hunted down and secured, with Jupiter's assistance, a scarabaeus which he believed to be totally new, but in respect to which he wished to have my opinion on the morrow.

"And why not to-night?" I asked, rubbing my hands over the blaze, and wishing the whole tribe of scarabaei at the devil.

"Ah, if I had only known you were here!" said Legrand, "but it's so long since I saw you; and how could I foresee that you would pay me a visit this very night of all others? As I was coming home I met Lieutenant G----, from the fort, and, very foolishly, I lent him the bug; so it will be impossible for you to see it until the morning. Stay here to-night, and I will send Jup down for it at sunrise. It is the loveliest thing in creation!"

"What?--sunrise?"

"Nonsense! no!--the bug. It is of a brilliant gold color--about the size of a large hickory nut--with two jet black spots near one extremity of the back, and another, somewhat longer, at the other. The antennae are --"

"Dey ain't NO tin in him, Massa Will, I keep a tellin' on you," here interrupted Jupiter; "de bug is a goole-bug, solid, ebery bit of him, inside and all, sep him wing--neber feel half so hebby a bug in my life."

"Well, suppose it is, Jup," replied Legrand, somewhat more earnestly, it seemed to me, than the case demanded; "is that any reason for your letting the birds burn? The color"--here he turned to me-- "is really almost enough to warrant Jupiter's idea. You never saw a more brilliant metallic luster than the scales emit--but of this you cannot judge till to-morrow. In the meantime I can give you some idea of the shape." Saying this, he seated himself at a small table, on which were a pen and ink, but no paper. He looked for some in a drawer, but found none.

"Never mind," he said at length, "this will answer;" and he drew from his waistcoat pocket a scrap of what I took to be very dirty foolscap, and made upon it a rough drawing with the pen. While he did this, I retained my seat by the fire, for I was still chilly. When the design was complete, he handed it to me without rising. As I received it, a loud growl was heard, succeeded by a scratching at the door. Jupiter opened it, and a large Newfoundland, belonging to Legrand, rushed in, leaped upon my shoulders, and loaded me with caresses; for I had shown him much attention during previous visits. When his gambols were over, I looked at the paper, and, to speak the truth, found myself not a little puzzled at what my friend had depicted.

"Well!" I said, after contemplating it for some minutes, "this IS a strange scarabaeus, I must confess; new to me; never saw anything like it before--unless it was a skull, or a death's head, which it more nearly resembles than anything else that has come under MY observation."

"A death's head!" echoed Legrand. "Oh--yes--well, it has something of that appearance upon paper, no doubt. The two upper black spots look like eyes, eh? and the longer one at the bottom like a mouth-- and then the shape of the whole is oval."

"Perhaps so," said I; "but, Legrand, I fear you are no artist. I must wait until I see the beetle itself, if I am to form any idea of its personal appearance."

"Well, I don't know," said he, a little nettled, "I draw tolerably--SHOULD do it at least--have had good masters, and flatter myself that I am not quite a blockhead."

"But, my dear fellow, you are joking then," said I, "this is a very passable SKULL--indeed, I may say that it is a very EXCELLENT skull, according to the vulgar notions about such specimens of physiology--and your scarabaeus must be the queerest scarabaeus in the world if it resembles it. Why, we may get up a very thrilling bit of superstition upon this hint. I presume you will call the bug Scarabaeus caput hominis, or something of that kind--there are many similar titles in the Natural Histories. But where are the antennae you spoke of?"

"The antennae!" said Legrand, who seemed to be getting unaccountably warm upon the subject; "I am sure you must see the antennae. I made them as distinct as they are in the original insect, and I presume that is sufficient."

"Well, well," I said, "perhaps you have--still I don't see them;" and I handed him the paper without additional remark, not wishing to ruffle his temper; but I was much surprised at the turn affairs had taken; his ill humor puzzled me-

-and, as for the drawing of the beetle, there were positively NO antennae visible, and the whole DID bear a very close resemblance to the ordinary cuts of a death's head.

He received the paper very peevishly, and was about to crumple it, apparently to throw it in the fire, when a casual glance at the design seemed suddenly to rivet his attention. In an instant his face grew violently red--in another excessively pale. For some minutes he continued to scrutinize the drawing minutely where he sat. At length he arose, took a candle from the table, and proceeded to seat himself upon a sea chest in the farthest corner of the room. Here again he made an anxious examination of the paper, turning it in all directions. He said nothing, however, and his conduct greatly astonished me; yet I thought it prudent not to exacerbate the growing moodiness of his temper by any comment. Presently he took from his coat pocket a wallet, placed the paper carefully in it, and deposited both in a writing desk, which he locked. He now grew more composed in his demeanor; but his original air of enthusiasm had quite disappeared. Yet he seemed not so much sulky as abstracted. As the evening wore away he became more and more absorbed in reverie, from which no sallies of mine could arouse him. It had been my intention to pass the night at the hut, as I had frequently done before, but, seeing my host in this mood, I deemed it proper to take leave. He did not press me to remain, but, as I departed, he shook my hand with even more than his usual cordiality.

It was about a month after this (and during the interval I had seen nothing of Legrand) when I received a visit, at Charleston, from his man, Jupiter. I had never seen the good old negro look so dispirited, and I feared that some serious disaster had befallen my friend.

"Well, Jup," said I, "what is the matter now?--how is your master?"

"Why, to speak the troof, massa, him not so berry well as mought be."

"Not well! I am truly sorry to hear it. What does he complain of?"

"Dar! dot's it!--him neber 'plain of notin'--but him berry sick for all dat."

"VERY sick, Jupiter!--why didn't you say so at once? Is he confined to bed?"

"No, dat he aint!--he aint 'fin'd nowhar--dat's just whar de shoe pinch--my mind is got to be berry hebby 'bout poor Massa Will."

"Jupiter, I should like to understand what it is you are talking about. You say your master is sick. Hasn't he told you what ails him?"

"Why, massa, 'taint worf while for to git mad about de matter--Massa Will say noffin at all aint de matter wid him--but den what make him go about looking dis here way, wid he head down and he soldiers up, and as white as a goose? And den he keep a syphon all de time—"

"Keeps a what, Jupiter?"

"Keeps a syphon wid de figgurs on de slate--de queerest figgurs I ebber did see. Ise gittin' to be skeered, I tell you. Hab for to keep mighty tight eye 'pon him 'noovers. Todder day he gib me slip 'fore de sun up and was gone de whole ob de blessed day. I had a big stick ready cut for to gib him deuced good beating when he did come--but Ise sich a fool dat I hadn't de heart arter all--he looked so berry poorly."

"Eh?--what?--ah yes!--upon the whole I think you had better not be too severe with the poor fellow--don't flog him, Jupiter--he can't very well stand it--but can you form no idea of what has occasioned this illness, or rather this change of conduct? Has anything unpleasant happened since I saw you?"

"No, massa, dey aint bin noffin onpleasant SINCE den—'twas 'FORE den I'm feared--'twas de berry day you was dare."

"How? what do you mean?"

"Why, massa, I mean de bug--dare now."

"The what?"

"De bug--I'm berry sartin dat Massa Will bin bit somewhere 'bout de head by dat goole-bug."

"And what cause have you, Jupiter, for such a supposition?"

"Claws enuff, massa, and mouff, too. I nebber did see sich a deuced bug--he kick and he bite eberyting what cum near him. Massa Will cotch him fuss, but had for to let him go 'gin mighty quick, I tell you--den was de time he must ha' got de bite. I didn't like de look ob de bug mouff, myself, nohow, so I wouldn't take hold oh him wid my finger, but I cotch him wid a piece oh paper dat I found. I rap him up in de paper and stuff a piece of it in he mouff--dat was de way."

"And you think, then, that your master was really bitten by the beetle, and that the bite made him sick?"

"I don't think noffin about it--I nose it. What make him dream 'bout de goole so much, if 'taint cause he bit by the goole-bug? Ise heered 'bout dem goole-bugs 'fore dis."

"But how do you know he dreams about gold?"

"How I know? why, 'cause he talk about it in he sleep--dat's how I nose."

"Well, Jup, perhaps you are right; but to what fortunate circumstance am I to attribute the honor of a visit from you to- day?"

"What de matter, massa?"

"Did you bring any message from Mr. Legrand?"

"No, massa, I bring dis here pissel;" and here Jupiter handed me a note which ran thus:

MY DEAR ----

Why have I not seen you for so long a time? I hope you have not been so foolish as to take offense at any little brusquerie of mine; but no, that is improbable.

Since I saw you I have had great cause for anxiety. I have something to tell you, yet scarcely know how to tell it, or whether I should tell it at all.

I have not been quite well for some days past, and poor old Jup annoys me, almost beyond endurance, by his well-meant attentions. Would you believe it?--he had prepared a huge stick, the other day, with which to chastise me for giving him the slip, and spending the day, solus, among the hills on the mainland. I verily believe that my ill looks alone saved me a flogging.

I have made no addition to my cabinet since we met. If you can, in any way, make it convenient, come over with Jupiter. DO come. I wish to see you TO-NIGHT, upon business of importance. I assure you that it is of the HIGHEST importance.

Ever yours,

WILLIAM LEGRAND

There was something in the tone of this note which gave me great uneasiness. Its whole style differed materially from that of Legrand. What could he be dreaming of? What new crotchet possessed his excitable brain? What "business of the highest importance" could HE possibly have to transact? Jupiter's account of him boded no good. I dreaded lest the continued pressure of misfortune had, at length, fairly unsettled the reason of my friend. Without a moment's hesitation, therefore, I prepared to accompany the negro.

Upon reaching the wharf, I noticed a scythe and three spades, all apparently new, lying in the bottom of the boat in which we were to embark.

"What is the meaning of all this, Jup?" I inquired.

"Him syfe, massa, and spade."

"Very true; but what are they doing here?"

"Him de syfe and de spade what Massa Will sis 'pon my buying for him in de town, and de debbil's own lot of money I had to gib for em."

"But what, in the name of all that is mysterious, is your 'Massa Will' going to do with scythes and spades?"

"Dat's more dan I know, and debbil take me if I don't b'lieve 'tis more dan he know too. But it's all cum ob de bug."

Finding that no satisfaction was to be obtained of Jupiter, whose whole intellect seemed to be absorbed by "de bug," I now stepped into the boat, and made sail. With a fair and strong breeze we soon ran into the little cove to the northward of Fort Moultrie, and a walk of some two miles brought us to the hut. It was about three in the afternoon when we arrived. Legrand had been awaiting us in eager expectation. He grasped my hand with a nervous empressement which alarmed me and strengthened the suspicions already entertained. His countenance was pale even to ghastliness, and his deep-set eyes glared with unnatural luster. After some inquiries respecting his health, I asked him, not knowing what better to say, if he had yet obtained the scarabaeus from Lieutenant G.

"Oh, yes," he replied, coloring violently, "I got it from him the next morning. Nothing should tempt me to part with that scarabaeus. Do you know that Jupiter is quite right about it?"

"In what way?" I asked, with a sad foreboding at heart.

"In supposing it to be a bug of REAL GOLD." He said this with an air of profound seriousness, and I felt inexpressibly shocked.

"This bug is to make my fortune," he continued, with a triumphant smile; "to reinstate me in my family possessions. Is it any wonder, then, that I prize it? Since Fortune has thought fit to bestow it upon me, I have only to use it properly, and I shall arrive at the gold of which it is the index. Jupiter, bring me that scarabaeus!"

"What! de bug, massa? I'd rudder not go fer trubble dat bug; you mus' git him for your own self."

Hereupon Legrand arose, with a grave and stately air, and brought me the beetle from a glass case in which it was enclosed. It was a beautiful scarabaeus, and, at that time, unknown to naturalists--of course a great prize in a scientific point of view. There were two round black spots near one extremity of the back, and a long one near the other. The scales were exceedingly hard and glossy, with all the appearance of burnished gold. The weight of the insect was very remarkable, and, taking all things into consideration, I could hardly blame Jupiter for his opinion respecting it; but what to make of Legrand's concordance with that opinion, I could not, for the life of me, tell.

"I sent for you," said he, in a grandiloquent tone, when I had completed my examination of the beetle, "I sent for you that I might have your counsel and assistance in furthering the views of Fate and of the bug."

"My dear Legrand," I cried, interrupting him, "you are certainly unwell, and had better use some little precautions. You shall go to bed, and I will remain with you a few days, until you get over this. You are feverish and --"

"Feel my pulse," said he.

I felt it, and, to say the truth, found not the slightest indication of fever.

"But you may be ill and yet have no fever. Allow me this once to prescribe for you. In the first place go to bed. In the next --"

"You are mistaken," he interposed, "I am as well as I can expect to be under the excitement which I suffer. If you really wish me well, you will relieve this excitement."

"And how is this to be done?"

"Very easily. Jupiter and myself are going upon an expedition into the hills, upon the mainland, and, in this expedition, we shall need the aid of some person in whom we can confide. You are the only one we can trust. Whether we succeed or fail, the excitement which you now perceive in me will be equally allayed."

"I am anxious to oblige you in any way," I replied; "but do you mean to say that this infernal beetle has any connection with your expedition into the hills?"

"It has."

"Then, Legrand, I can become a party to no such absurd proceeding."

"I am sorry--very sorry--for we shall have to try it by ourselves."

"Try it by yourselves! The man is surely mad!--but stay!--how long do you propose to be absent?"

"Probably all night. We shall start immediately, and be back, at all events, by sunrise."

"And will you promise me, upon your honor, that when this freak of yours is over, and the bug business (good God!) settled to your satisfaction, you will then return home and follow my advice implicitly, as that of your physician?"

"Yes; I promise; and now let us be off, for we have no time to lose."

With a heavy heart I accompanied my friend. We started about four o'clock--Legrand, Jupiter, the dog, and myself. Jupiter had with him the scythe and spades--the whole of which he insisted upon carrying--more through fear, it seemed to me, of trusting either of the implements within reach of his master, than from any excess of industry or complaisance. His demeanor was dogged in the extreme, and "dat deuced bug" were the sole words which escaped his lips during the journey.

For my own part, I had charge of a couple of dark lanterns, while Legrand contented himself with the scarabaeus, which he carried attached to the end of a bit of whipcord; twirling it to and fro, with the air of a conjurer, as he went. When I observed this last, plain evidence of my friend's aberration of mind, I could scarcely refrain from tears. I thought it best, however, to humor his fancy, at least for the present, or until I could adopt some more energetic measures with a chance of success. In the meantime I endeavored, but all in vain, to sound him in regard to the object of the expedition. Having succeeded in inducing me to accompany him, he seemed unwilling to hold conversation upon any topic of minor importance, and to all my questions vouchsafed no other reply than "we shall see!"

We crossed the creek at the head of the island by means of a skiff, and, ascending the high grounds on the shore of the mainland, proceeded in a northwesterly direction, through a tract of country excessively wild and desolate, where no trace of a human footstep was to be seen. Legrand led the way with decision; pausing only for an instant, here and there, to consult what appeared to be certain landmarks of his own contrivance upon a former occasion.

In this manner we journeyed for about two hours, and the sun was just setting when we entered a region infinitely more dreary than any yet seen. It was a species of table-land, near the summit of an almost inaccessible hill, densely wooded from base to pinnacle, and interspersed with huge crags that appeared to lie loosely upon the soil, and in many cases were prevented from precipitating themselves into the valleys below, merely by the support of the trees against which they reclined. Deep ravines, in various directions, gave an air of still sterner solemnity to the scene.

The natural platform to which we had clambered was thickly overgrown with brambles, through which we soon discovered that it would have been impossible to force our way but for the scythe; and Jupiter, by direction of his master, proceeded to clear for us a path to the foot of an enormously tall tulip tree, which stood, with some eight or ten oaks, upon the level, and far surpassed them all, and all other trees which I had then ever seen, in the beauty of its foliage and form, in the wide spread of its branches, and in the general majesty of its appearance. When we reached this tree, Legrand turned to Jupiter, and asked him if he thought he could climb it. The old man seemed a little staggered by the question, and for some moments made no reply. At length he approached the huge trunk, walked slowly around it, and examined it with minute attention. When he had completed his scrutiny, he merely said:

"Yes, massa, Jup climb any tree he ebber see in he life.'"

"Then up with you as soon as possible, for it will soon be too dark to see what we are about."

"How far mus' go up, massa?" inquired Jupiter.

"Get up the main trunk first, and then I will tell you which way to go--and here--stop! take this beetle with you."

"De bug, Massa Will!--de goole-bug!" cried the negro, drawing back in dismay—"what for mus' tote de bug way up de tree?--d--n if I do!"

"If you are afraid, Jup, a great big negro like you, to take hold of a harmless little dead beetle, why you can carry it up by this string--but, if you do not take it up with you in some way, I shall be under the necessity of breaking your head with this shovel."

"What de matter now, massa?" said Jup, evidently shamed into compliance; "always want for to raise fuss wid old nigger. Was only funnin anyhow. ME feered de bug! what I keer for de bug?" Here he took cautiously hold of the extreme end of the string, and, maintaining the insect as far from his person as circumstances would permit, prepared to ascend the tree.

In youth, the tulip tree, or Liriodendron tulipiferum, the most magnificent of American foresters, has a trunk peculiarly smooth, and often rises to a great height without lateral branches; but, in its riper age, the bark becomes gnarled and uneven, while many short limbs make their appearance on the stem. Thus the difficulty of ascension, in the present case, lay more in semblance than in reality. Embracing the huge cylinder, as closely as possible, with his arms and knees, seizing with his hands some projections, and resting his naked toes upon others, Jupiter, after one or two narrow escapes from falling, at length wriggled himself into the first great fork, and seemed to consider the whole business as virtually accomplished. The RISK of the achievement was, in fact, now over, although the climber was some sixty or seventy feet from the ground.

"Which way mus' go now, Massa Will?" he asked.

"Keep up the largest branch--the one on this side," said Legrand. The negro obeyed him promptly, and apparently with but little trouble; ascending higher and higher, until no glimpse of his squat figure could be obtained through the dense foliage which enveloped it. Presently his voice was heard in a sort of halloo.

"How much fudder is got to go?"

"How high up are you?" asked Legrand.

"Ebber so fur," replied the negro; "can see de sky fru de top oh de tree."

"Never mind the sky, but attend to what I say. Look down the trunk and count the limbs below you on this side. How many limbs have you passed?"

"One, two, tree, four, fibe--I done pass fibe big limb, massa, 'pon dis side."

"Then go one limb higher."

In a few minutes the voice was heard again, announcing that the seventh limb was attained.

"Now, Jup," cried Legrand, evidently much excited, "I want you to work your way out upon that limb as far as you can. If you see anything strange let me know."

By this time what little doubt I might have entertained of my poor friend's insanity was put finally at rest. I had no alternative but to conclude him stricken with lunacy, and I became seriously anxious about getting him home. While I was pondering upon what was best to be done, Jupiter's voice was again heard.

"Mos feered for to ventur pon dis limb berry far--'tis dead limb putty much all de way."

"Did you say it was a DEAD limb, Jupiter?" cried Legrand in a quavering voice.

"Yes, massa, him dead as de door-nail--done up for sartin--done departed dis here life."

"What in the name of heaven shall I do?" asked Legrand, seemingly in the greatest distress.

"Do!" said I, glad of an opportunity to interpose a word, "why come home and go to bed. Come now!--that's a fine fellow. It's getting late, and, besides, you remember your promise."

"Jupiter," cried he, without heeding me in the least, "do you hear me?"

"Yes, Massa Will, hear you ebber so plain."

"Try the wood well, then, with your knife, and see if you think it VERY rotten."

"Him rotten, massa, sure nuff," replied the negro in a few moments, "but not so berry rotten as mought be. Mought venture out leetle way pon de limb by myself, dat's true."

"By yourself!--what do you mean?"

"Why, I mean de bug. 'Tis BERRY hebby bug. Spose I drop him down fuss, an den de limb won't break wid just de weight of one nigger."

"You infernal scoundrel!" cried Legrand, apparently much relieved, "what do you mean by telling me such nonsense as that? As sure as you drop that beetle I'll break your neck. Look here, Jupiter, do you hear me?"

"Yes, massa, needn't hollo at poor nigger dat style."

"Well! now listen!--if you will venture out on the limb as far as you think safe, and not let go the beetle, I'll make you a present of a silver dollar as soon as you get down."

"I'm gwine, Massa Will--deed I is," replied the negro very promptly—"mos out to the end now."

"OUT TO THE END!" here fairly screamed Legrand; "do you say you are out to the end of that limb?"

"Soon be to de end, massa--o-o-o-o-oh! Lor-gol-a-marcy! what IS dis here pon de tree?"

"Well!" cried Legrand, highly delighted, "what is it?"

"Why 'taint noffin but a skull--somebody bin lef him head up de tree, and de crows done gobble ebery bit ob de meat off."

"A skull, you say!--very well,--how is it fastened to the limb?-- what holds it on?"

"Sure nuff, massa; mus look. Why dis berry curious sarcumstance, pon my word--dare's a great big nail in de skull, what fastens ob it on to de tree."

"Well now, Jupiter, do exactly as I tell you--do you hear?"

"Yes, massa."

"Pay attention, then--find the left eye of the skull."

"Hum! hoo! Dat's good! why dey ain't no eye lef at all."

"Curse your stupidity! do you know your right hand from your left?"

"Yes, I knows dat--knows all about dat—'tis my lef hand what I chops de wood wid."

"To be sure! you are left-handed; and your left eye is on the same side as your left hand.

Now, I suppose, you can find the left eye of the skull, or the place where the left eye has been. Have you found it?"

Here was a long pause. At length the negro asked:

"Is de lef eye of de skull pon de same side as de lef hand of de skull too?--cause de skull aint got not a bit oh a hand at all-- nebber mind! I got de lef eye now--here de lef eye! what mus do wid it?"

"Let the beetle drop through it, as far as the string will reach-- but be careful and not let go your hold of the string."

"All dat done, Massa Will; mighty easy ting for to put de bug fru de hole--look out for him dare below!"

During this colloquy no portion of Jupiter's person could be seen; but the beetle, which he had suffered to descend, was now visible at the end of the string, and glistened, like a globe of burnished gold, in the last rays of the setting sun, some of which still faintly illumined the eminence upon which we stood. The scarabaeus hung quite clear of any branches, and, if allowed to fall, would have fallen at our feet. Legrand immediately took the scythe, and cleared with it a circular space, three or four yards in diameter, just beneath the insect, and, having accomplished this, ordered Jupiter to let go the string and come down from the tree.

Driving a peg, with great nicety, into the ground, at the precise spot where the beetle fell, my friend now produced from his pocket a tape measure. Fastening one end of this at that point of the trunk of the tree which was nearest the peg, he unrolled it till it reached the peg and thence further unrolled it, in the direction already established by the two points of the tree and the peg, for the distance of fifty feet--Jupiter clearing away the brambles with the scythe. At the spot thus attained a second peg was driven, and about this, as a center, a rude circle, about four feet in diameter, described. Taking now a spade himself, and giving one to Jupiter and one to me, Legrand begged us to set about digging as quickly as possible.

To speak the truth, I had no especial relish for such amusement at any time, and, at that particular moment, would willingly have declined it; for the night was coming on, and I felt much fatigued with the exercise already taken; but I saw no mode of escape, and was fearful of disturbing my poor friend's equanimity by a refusal. Could I have depended, indeed, upon Jupiter's aid, I would have had no hesitation in attempting to get the lunatic home by force; but I was too well assured of the old negro's disposition, to hope that he would assist me, under any circumstances, in a personal contest with his master. I made no doubt that the latter had been infected with some of the innumerable Southern superstitions about money buried, and that his fantasy had received confirmation by the finding of the scarabaeus, or, perhaps, by Jupiter's obstinacy in maintaining it to be "a bug of real gold." A mind disposed to lunacy would readily be led away by such suggestions--especially if chiming in with favorite preconceived ideas--and then I called to mind the poor fellow's speech about the beetle's being "the index of his fortune." Upon the whole, I was sadly vexed and puzzled, but, at length, I concluded to make a virtue of necessity--to dig with a good will, and thus the sooner to convince the visionary, by ocular demonstration, of the fallacy of the opinion he entertained.

The lanterns having been lit, we all fell to work with a zeal worthy a more rational cause; and, as the glare fell upon our persons and implements, I could not help thinking how picturesque a group we composed, and how strange and suspicious our labors must have appeared to any interloper who, by chance, might have stumbled upon our whereabouts.

We dug very steadily for two hours. Little was said; and our chief embarrassment lay in the yelpings of the dog, who took exceeding interest in our proceedings. He, at length, became so obstreperous that we grew fearful of his giving the alarm to some stragglers in the vicinity,--or, rather, this was the apprehension of Legrand;-- for myself, I should have rejoiced at any interruption which might have enabled me to get the wanderer home. The noise was, at length, very effectually silenced by Jupiter, who, getting out of the hole with a dogged air of deliberation, tied the brute's mouth up with one of his suspenders, and then returned, with a grave chuckle, to his task.

When the time mentioned had expired, we had reached a depth of five feet, and yet no signs of any treasure became manifest. A general pause ensued, and I began to hope that the farce was at an end. Legrand, however, although evidently much disconcerted, wiped his brow thoughtfully and recommenced. We had excavated the entire circle of four feet diameter, and now we slightly enlarged the limit, and went to the farther depth of two feet. Still nothing appeared. The gold-seeker, whom I sincerely pitied, at length clambered from the pit, with the bitterest disappointment imprinted upon every feature, and proceeded, slowly and reluctantly, to put on his coat, which he had thrown off at the beginning of his labor. In the meantime I made no remark. Jupiter, at a signal from his master, began to gather up his tools. This done, and the dog having been unmuzzled, we turned in profound silence toward home.

We had taken, perhaps, a dozen steps in this direction, when, with a loud oath, Legrand strode up to Jupiter, and seized him by the collar. The astonished negro opened his eyes and mouth to the fullest extent, let fall the spades, and fell upon his knees.

"You scoundrel!" said Legrand, hissing out the syllables from between his clenched teeth— "you infernal black villain!--speak, I tell you!--answer me this instant, without prevarication!--which-- which is your left eye."

"Oh, my golly, Massa Will! aint dis here my lef eye for sartain?" roared the terrified Jupiter, placing his hand upon his RIGHT organ of vision, and holding it there with a desperate pertinacity, as if in immediate, dread of his master's attempt at a gouge.

"I thought so!--I knew it! hurrah!" vociferated Legrand, letting the negro go and executing a series of curvets and caracols, much to the astonishment of his valet, who, arising from his knees, looked, mutely, from his master to myself, and then from myself to his master.

"Come! we must go back," said the latter, "the game's not up yet;" and he again led the way to the tulip tree.

"Jupiter," said he, when we reached its foot, "come here! was the skull nailed to the limb with the face outward, or with the face to the limb?"

"De face was out, massa, so dat de crows could get at de eyes good, widout any trouble."

"Well, then, was it this eye or that through which you dropped the beetle?" here Legrand touched each of Jupiter's eyes.

"Twas dis eye, massa--de lef eye--jis as you tell me," and here it was his right eye that the negro indicated.

"That will do--we must try it again."

Here my friend, about whose madness I now saw, or fancied that I saw, certain indications of method, removed the peg which marked the spot where the beetle fell, to a spot about three inches to the westward of its former position. Taking, now, the tape measure from the nearest point of the trunk to the peg, as before, and continuing the extension in a straight line to the distance of fifty feet, a spot was indicated, removed, by several yards, from the point at which we had been digging.

Around the new position a circle, somewhat larger than in the former instance, was now described, and we again set to work with the spade. I was dreadfully weary, but, scarcely understanding what had occasioned the change in my thoughts, I felt no longer any great aversion from the labor imposed. I had become most unaccountably interested--nay, even excited. Perhaps there was something, amid all the extravagant demeanor of Legrand--some air of forethought, or of deliberation, which impressed me. I dug eagerly, and now and then caught myself actually looking, with something that very much resembled expectation, for the fancied treasure, the vision of which had demented my unfortunate companion. At a period when such vagaries of thought most fully possessed me, and when we had been at work perhaps an hour and a half, we were again interrupted by the violent howlings of the dog. His uneasiness, in the first instance, had been, evidently, but the result of playfulness or caprice, but he now assumed a bitter and serious tone. Upon Jupiter's again attempting to muzzle him, he made furious resistance, and, leaping into the hole, tore up the mold frantically with his claws. In a few seconds he had uncovered a mass of human bones, forming two complete skeletons, intermingled with several buttons of metal, and what appeared to be the dust of decayed woolen. One or two strokes of a spade upturned the blade of a large Spanish knife, and, as we dug farther, three or four loose pieces of gold and silver coin came to light.

At sight of these the joy of Jupiter could scarcely be restrained, but the countenance of his master wore an air of extreme disappointment. He urged us, however, to continue our exertions, and the words were hardly uttered when I stumbled and fell forward, having caught the toe of my boot in a large ring of iron that lay half buried in the loose earth.

We now worked in earnest, and never did I pass ten minutes of more intense excitement. During this interval we had fairly unearthed an oblong chest of wood, which, from its perfect preservation and wonderful hardness, had plainly been subjected to some mineralizing process--perhaps that of the bichloride of mercury. This box was three feet and a half long, three feet broad, and two and a half feet deep. It was firmly secured by bands of wrought iron, riveted, and forming a kind of open trelliswork over the whole. On each side of the chest, near the top, were three rings of iron--six in all--by means of which a firm hold could be obtained by six persons. Our utmost united endeavors served only to disturb the coffer very slightly in its bed. We at once saw the impossibility of removing so great a weight. Luckily, the sole fastenings of the lid consisted of two sliding bolts. These we drew back--trembling and panting with anxiety. In an instant, a treasure of incalculable value lay gleaming before us. As the rays of the lanterns fell within the pit, there flashed upward a glow and a glare, from a confused heap of gold and of jewels, that absolutely dazzled our eyes.

I shall not pretend to describe the feelings with which I gazed. Amazement was, of course, predominant. Legrand appeared exhausted with excitement, and spoke very few words. Jupiter's countenance wore, for some minutes, as deadly a pallor as it is possible, in the nature of things, for any negro's visage to assume. He seemed stupefied--thunderstricken. Presently he fell upon his knees in the pit, and burying his naked arms up to the elbows in gold, let them there remain, as if enjoying the luxury of a bath. At length, with a deep sigh, he exclaimed, as if in a soliloquy:

"And dis all cum of de goole-bug! de putty goole-bug! de poor little goole-bug, what I boosed in that sabage kind oh style! Ain't you shamed oh yourself, nigger?--answer me dat!"

It became necessary, at last, that I should arouse both master and valet to the expediency of removing the treasure. It was growing late, and it behooved us to make exertion, that we might get everything housed before daylight. It was difficult to say what should be done, and much time was spent in deliberation--so confused were the ideas of all. We, finally, lightened the box by removing two thirds of its contents, when we were enabled, with some trouble, to raise it from the hole. The articles taken out were deposited among the brambles, and the dog left to guard them, with strict orders from Jupiter neither, upon any pretense, to stir from the spot, nor to open his mouth until our return. We then hurriedly made for home with the chest; reaching the hut in safety, but after excessive toil, at one o'clock in the morning. Worn out as we were, it was not in human nature to do more immediately. We rested until two, and had supper; starting for the hills immediately afterwards, armed with three stout sacks, which, by good luck, were upon the premises. A little before four we arrived at the pit, divided the remainder of the booty, as equally as might be, among us, and, leaving the holes unfilled, again set out for the hut, at which, for the second time, we deposited our golden burdens, just as the first faint streaks of the dawn gleamed from over the treetops in the east.

We were now thoroughly broken down; but the intense excitement of the time denied us repose. After an unquiet slumber of some three or four hours' duration, we arose, as if by preconcert, to make examination of our treasure.

The chest had been full to the brim, and we spent the whole day, and the greater part of the next night, in a scrutiny of its contents. There had been nothing like order or arrangement. Everything had been heaped in promiscuously. Having assorted all with care, we found ourselves possessed of even vaster wealth than we had at first supposed. In coin there was rather more than four hundred and fifty thousand dollars--estimating the value of the pieces, as accurately as we could, by the tables of the period. There was not a particle of silver. All was gold of antique date and of great variety--French, Spanish, and German money, with a few English guineas, and some counters, of which we had never seen specimens before. There were several very large and heavy coins, so worn that we could make nothing of their inscriptions. There was no American money. The value of the jewels we found more difficulty in estimating. There were diamonds--some of them exceedingly large and fine--a hundred and ten in all, and not one of them small; eighteen rubies of remarkable brilliancy;--three hundred and ten emeralds, all very beautiful; and twenty-one sapphires, with an opal. These stones had all been broken from their settings and thrown loose in the chest. The settings themselves, which we picked out from among the other gold, appeared to have been beaten up with hammers, as if to prevent identification. Besides all this, there was a vast quantity of solid gold ornaments; nearly two hundred massive finger and ears rings; rich chains--thirty of these, if I remember; eighty-three very large and heavy crucifixes; five gold censers of great value; a prodigious golden punch bowl, ornamented with richly chased vine leaves and Bacchanalian figures; with two sword handles exquisitely embossed, and many other smaller articles which I cannot recollect. The weight of these valuables exceeded three hundred and fifty pounds avoirdupois; and in this estimate I have not included one hundred and ninety-seven superb gold watches; three of the number being worth each five hundred dollars, if one. Many of them were very old, and as timekeepers valueless; the works having suffered, more or less, from corrosion--but all were richly jeweled and in cases of great worth. We estimated the entire contents of the chest, that night, at a million and a half of dollars; and upon the subsequent disposal of the trinkets and jewels (a few being retained for our own use), it was found that we had greatly undervalued the treasure.

When, at length, we had concluded our examination, and the intense excitement of the time had, in some measure, subsided, Legrand, who saw that I was dying with impatience for a solution of this most extraordinary riddle, entered into a full detail of all the circumstances connected with it.

“You remember,” said he, “the night when I handed you the rough sketch I had made of the scarabaeus. You recollect, also, that I became quite vexed at you for insisting that my drawing resembled a death's head. When you first made this assertion I thought you were jesting; but afterwards I called to mind the peculiar spots on the back of the insect, and admitted to myself that your remark had some little foundation in fact. Still, the sneer at my graphic powers irritated me--for I am considered a good artist--

and, therefore, when you handed me the scrap of parchment, I was about to crumple it up and throw it angrily into the fire."

"The scrap of paper, you mean," said I.

"No; it had much of the appearance of paper, and at first I supposed it to be such, but when I came to draw upon it, I discovered it at once to be a piece of very thin parchment. It was quite dirty, you remember. Well, as I was in the very act of crumpling it up, my glance fell upon the sketch at which you had been looking, and you may imagine my astonishment when I perceived, in fact, the figure of a death's head just where, it seemed to me, I had made the drawing of the beetle. For a moment I was too much amazed to think with accuracy. I knew that my design was very different in detail from this--although there was a certain similarity in general outline. Presently I took a candle, and seating myself at the other end of the room, proceeded to scrutinize the parchment more closely. Upon turning it over, I saw my own sketch upon the reverse, just as I had made it. My first idea, now, was mere surprise at the really remarkable similarity of outline--at the singular coincidence involved in the fact that, unknown to me, there should have been a skull upon the other side of the parchment, immediately beneath my figure of the scarabaeus, and that this skull, not only in outline, but in size, should so closely resemble my drawing. I say the singularity of this coincidence absolutely stupefied me for a time.

This is the usual effect of such coincidences. The mind struggles to establish a connection--a sequence of cause and effect--and, being unable to do so, suffers a species of temporary paralysis. But, when I recovered from this stupor, there dawned upon me gradually a conviction which startled me even far more than the coincidence. I began distinctly, positively, to remember that there had been NO drawing upon the parchment, when I made my sketch of the scarabaeus. I became perfectly certain of this; for I recollected turning up first one side and then the other, in search of the cleanest spot. Had the skull been then there, of course I could not have failed to notice it. Here was indeed a mystery which I felt it impossible to explain; but, even at that early moment, there seemed to glimmer, faintly, within the most remote and secret chambers of my intellect, a glow-wormlike conception of that truth which last night's adventure brought to so magnificent a demonstration. I arose at once, and putting the parchment securely away, dismissed all further reflection until I should be alone.

"When you had gone, and when Jupiter was fast asleep, I betook myself to a more methodical investigation of the affair. In the first place I considered the manner in which the parchment had come into my possession. The spot where we discovered the scarabaeus was on the coast of the mainland, about a mile eastward of the island, and but a short distance above high-water mark. Upon my taking hold of it, it gave me a sharp bite, which caused me to let it drop.

Jupiter, with his accustomed caution, before seizing the insect, which had flown toward him, looked about him for a leaf, or something of that nature, by which to take hold of it. It was at this moment that his eyes, and mine also, fell upon the scrap of parchment, which I then supposed to be paper. It was lying half buried in the sand, a corner sticking up. Near the spot where we found it, I observed the remnants of the hull of what appeared to have been a ship's longboat. The wreck seemed to have been there for a very great while, for the resemblance to boat timbers could scarcely be traced.

"Well, Jupiter picked up the parchment, wrapped the beetle in it, and gave it to me. Soon afterwards we turned to go home, and on the way met Lieutenant G----. I showed him the insect, and he begged me to let him take it to the fort. Upon my consenting, he thrust it forthwith into his waistcoat pocket, without the parchment in which it had been wrapped, and which I had continued to hold in my hand during his inspection. Perhaps he dreaded my changing my mind, and thought it best to make sure of the prize at once--you know how enthusiastic he is on all subjects connected with Natural History. At the same time, without being conscious of it, I must have deposited the parchment in my own pocket.

"You remember that when I went to the table, for the purpose of making a sketch of the beetle, I found no paper where it was usually kept. I looked in the drawer, and found none there. I searched my pockets, hoping to find an old letter, when my hand fell upon the parchment. I thus detail the precise mode in which it came into my possession, for the circumstances impressed me with peculiar force.

"No doubt you will think me fanciful--but I had already established a kind of CONNECTION. I had put together two links of a great chain. There was a boat lying upon a seacoast, and not far from the boat was a parchment--NOT A PAPER--with a skull depicted upon it. You will, of course, ask 'where is the connection?' I reply that the skull, or death's head, is the well-known emblem of the pirate. The flag of the death's head is hoisted in all engagements.

"I have said that the scrap was parchment, and not paper. Parchment is durable--almost imperishable. Matters of little moment are rarely consigned to parchment; since, for the mere ordinary purposes of drawing or writing, it is not nearly so well adapted as paper. This reflection suggested some meaning--some relevancy--in the death's head. I did not fail to observe, also, the FORM of the parchment. Although one of its corners had been, by some accident, destroyed, it could be seen that the original form was oblong. It was just such a slip, indeed, as might have been chosen for a memorandum--for a record of something to be long remembered, and carefully preserved."

"But," I interposed, "you say that the skull was NOT upon the parchment when you made the drawing of the beetle. How then do you trace any connection between the boat and the skull--since this latter, according to your own admission, must have been designed (God only knows how or by whom) at some period subsequent to your sketching the scarabaeus?"

"Ah, hereupon turns the whole mystery; although the secret, at this point, I had comparatively little difficulty in solving. My steps were sure, and could afford but a single result. I reasoned, for example, thus: When I drew the scarabaeus, there was no skull apparent upon the parchment. When I had completed the drawing I gave it to you, and observed you narrowly until you returned it. YOU, therefore, did not design the skull, and no one else was present to do it. Then it was not done by human agency. And nevertheless it was done.

"At this stage of my reflections I endeavored to remember, and DID remember, with entire distinctness, every incident which occurred about the period in question. The weather was chilly (oh, rare and happy accident!), and a fire was blazing upon the hearth. I was heated with exercise and sat near the table. You, however, had drawn a chair close to the chimney. Just as I placed the parchment in your hand, and as you were in the act of inspecting it, Wolf, the Newfoundland, entered, and leaped upon your shoulders. With your left hand you caressed him and kept him off, while your right, holding the parchment, was permitted to fall listlessly between your knees, and in close proximity to the fire. At one moment I thought the blaze had caught it, and was about to caution you, but, before I could speak, you had withdrawn it, and were engaged in its examination. When I considered all these particulars, I doubted not for a moment that HEAT had been the agent in bringing to light, upon the parchment, the skull which I saw designed upon it. You are well aware that chemical preparations exist, and have existed time out of mind, by means of which it is possible to write upon either paper or vellum, so that the characters shall become visible only when subjected to the action of fire. Zaffre, digested in aqua regia, and diluted with four times its weight of water, is sometimes employed; a green tint results. The regulus of cobalt, dissolved in spirit of niter, gives a red. These colors disappear at longer or shorter intervals after the material written upon cools, but again become apparent upon the reapplication of heat.

“I now scrutinized the death's head with care. Its outer edges-- the edges of the drawing nearest the edge of the vellum--were far more DISTINCT than the others. It was clear that the action of the caloric had been imperfect or unequal. I immediately kindled a fire, and subjected every portion of the parchment to a glowing heat. At first, the only effect was the strengthening of the faint lines in the skull; but, upon persevering in the experiment, there became visible, at the corner of the slip, diagonally opposite to the spot in which the death's head was delineated, the figure of what I at first supposed to be a goat. A closer scrutiny, however, satisfied me that it was intended for a kid."

"Ha! ha!" said I, "to be sure I have no right to laugh at you--a million and a half of money is too serious a matter for mirth--but you are not about to establish a third link in your chain--you will not find any especial connection between your pirates and a goat-- pirates, you know, have nothing to do with goats; they appertain to the farming interest."

"But I have just said that the figure was NOT that of a goat."

"Well, a kid then--pretty much the same thing."

"Pretty much, but not altogether," said Legrand. "You may have heard of one CAPTAIN Kidd. I at once looked upon the figure of the animal as a kind of punning or hieroglyphical signature. I say signature; because its position upon the vellum suggested this idea. The death's head at the corner diagonally opposite, had, in the same manner, the air of a stamp, or seal. But I was sorely put out by the absence of all else--of the body to my imagined instrument--of the text for my context."

"I presume you expected to find a letter between the stamp and the signature."

"Something of that kind. The fact is, I felt irresistibly impressed with a presentiment of some vast good fortune impending. I can scarcely say why. Perhaps, after all, it was rather a desire than an actual belief;--but do you know that Jupiter's silly words, about the bug being of solid gold, had a remarkable effect upon my fancy? And then the series of accidents and coincidents--these were so VERY extraordinary. Do you observe how mere an accident it was that these events should have occurred upon the SOLE day of all the year in which it has been, or may be sufficiently cool for fire, and that without the fire, or without the intervention of the dog at the precise moment in which he appeared, I should never have become aware of the death's head, and so never the possessor of the treasure?"

"But proceed--I am all impatience."

"Well; you have heard, of course, the many stories current--the thousand vague rumors afloat about money buried, somewhere upon the Atlantic coast, by Kidd and his associates. These rumors must have had some foundation in fact. And that the rumors have existed so long and so continuous, could have resulted, it appeared to me, only from the circumstance of the buried treasures still REMAINING entombed. Had Kidd concealed his plunder for a time, and afterwards reclaimed it, the rumors would scarcely have reached us in their present unvarying form. You will observe that the stories told are all about money-seekers, not about money-finders. Had the pirate recovered his money, there the affair would have dropped. It seemed to me that some accident--say the loss of a memorandum indicating its locality--had deprived him of the means of recovering it, and that this accident had become known to his followers, who otherwise might never have heard that the treasure had been concealed at all, and who, busying themselves in vain, because unguided, attempts to regain it, had given first birth, and then universal currency, to the reports which are now so common. Have you ever heard of any important treasure being unearthed along the coast?"

"Never."

"But that Kidd's accumulations were immense, is well known. I took it for granted, therefore, that the earth still held them; and you will scarcely be surprised when I tell you that I felt a hope, nearly amounting to certainty, that the parchment so strangely found involved a lost record of the place of deposit."

"But how did you proceed?"

"I held the vellum again to the fire, after increasing the heat, but nothing appeared. I now thought it possible that the coating of dirt might have something to do with the failure: so I carefully rinsed the parchment by pouring warm water over it, and, having done this, I placed it in a tin pan, with the skull downward, and put the pan upon a furnace of lighted charcoal. In a few minutes, the pan having become thoroughly heated, I removed the slip, and, to my inexpressible joy, found it spotted, in several places, with what appeared to be figures arranged in lines. Again I placed it in the pan, and suffered it to remain another minute. Upon taking it off, the whole was just as you see it now."

Here Legrand, having reheated the parchment, submitted it to my inspection. The following characters were rudely traced, in a red tint, between the death's head and the goat:

53++!305))6*;4826)4+)4+).;806*;48!8]60))85;1
+8*:+(;:+*8!83(88)5*!;

46(;88*96*?;8)*+(;485);5*!2:*+(;4956*2(5*-
4)8]8*;4069285);)6!8)4++;

1(+9;48081;8:8+1;48!85;4)485!528806*81(+9;4
8;(88;4(+?34;48)4+;161;:

188;+?;

"But," said I, returning him the slip, "I am as much in the dark as ever. Were all the jewels of Golconda awaiting me upon my solution of this enigma, I am quite sure that I should be unable to earn them."

"And yet," said Legrand, "the solution is by no means so difficult as you might be led to imagine from the first hasty inspection of the characters. These characters, as anyone might readily guess, form a cipher--that is to say, they convey a meaning; but then from what is known of Kidd, I could not suppose him capable of constructing any of the more abstruse cryptographs. I made up my mind, at once, that this was of a simple species--such, however, as would appear, to the crude intellect of the sailor, absolutely insoluble without the key."

"And you really solved it?"

"Readily; I have solved others of an abstruseness ten thousand times greater. Circumstances, and a certain bias of mind, have led me to take interest in such riddles, and it may well be doubted whether human ingenuity can construct an enigma of the kind which human ingenuity may not, by proper application, resolve. In fact, having once established connected and legible characters, I scarcely gave a thought to the mere difficulty of developing their import.

"In the present case--indeed in all cases of secret writing--the first question regards the LANGUAGE of the cipher; for the principles of solution, so far, especially, as the more simple ciphers are concerned, depend upon, and are varied by, the genius of the particular idiom. In general, there is no alternative but experiment (directed by probabilities) of every tongue known to him who attempts the solution, until the true one be attained. But, with the cipher now before us, all difficulty was removed by the signature. The pun upon the word 'Kidd' is appreciable in no other language than the English. But for this consideration I should have begun my attempts with the Spanish and French, as the tongues in which a secret of this kind would most naturally have been written by a pirate of the Spanish main. As it was, I assumed the cryptograph to be English.

"You observe there are no divisions between the words. Had there been divisions the task would have been comparatively easy. In such cases I should have commenced with a collation and analysis of the shorter words, and, had a word of a single letter occurred, as is most likely, (a or I, for example,) I should have considered the solution as assured. But, there being no division, my first step was to ascertain the predominant letters, as well as the least frequent. Counting all, I constructed a table thus:

Of the character 8 there are 33.

| | | |
|---|---|---|
| ; | " | 26. |
| 4 | " | 19. |
| +) | " | 16. |
| * | " | 13. |
| 5 | " | 12. |
| 6 | " | 11. |
| !1 | " | 8. |
| 0 | " | 6. |
| 92 | " | 5. |
| :3 | " | 4. |
| ? | " | 3. |
| ] | " | 2. |
| -. | " | 1. |

"Now, in English, the letter which most frequently occurs is e. Afterwards, the succession runs thus: a o i d h n r s t u y c f g l m w b k p q x z. E predominates so remarkably, that an individual sentence of any length is rarely seen, in which it is not the prevailing character.

"Here, then, we have, in the very beginning, the groundwork for something more than a mere guess. The general use which may be made of the table is obvious--but, in this particular cipher, we shall only very partially require its aid. As our predominant character is 8, we will commence by assuming it as the e of the natural alphabet. To verify the supposition, let us observe if the 8 be seen often in couples--for e is doubled with great frequency in English--in such words, for example, as 'meet,' 'fleet,' 'speed,' 'seen,' 'been,' 'agree,' etc. In the present instance we see it doubled no less than five times, although the cryptograph is brief.

"Let us assume 8, then, as e. Now, of all WORDS in the language, 'the' is most usual; let us see, therefore, whether there are not repetitions of any three characters, in the same order of collocation, the last of them being 8. If we discover repetitions of such letters, so arranged, they will most probably represent the word 'the.' Upon inspection, we find no less than seven such arrangements, the characters being ;48. We may, therefore, assume that ; represents t, 4 represents h, and 8 represents e--the last being now well confirmed. Thus a great step has been taken.

"But, having established a single word, we are enabled to establish a vastly important point; that is to say, several commencements and terminations of other words. Let us refer, for example, to the last instance but one, in which the combination ;48 occurs--not far from the end of the cipher. We know that the ; immediately ensuing is the commencement of a word, and, of the six characters succeeding this 'the,' we are cognizant of no less than five. Let us set these characters down, thus, by the letters we know them to represent, leaving a space for the unknown--

t eeth.

“Here we are enabled, at once, to discard the 'th,' as forming no portion of the word commencing with the first t; since, by experiment of the entire alphabet for a letter adapted to the vacancy, we perceive that no word can be formed of which this th can be a part. We are thus narrowed into

t ee,

and, going through the alphabet, if necessary, as before, we arrive at the word ‘tree,’ as the sole possible reading. We thus gain another letter, r, represented by (, with the words ‘the tree’ in juxtaposition.

“Looking beyond these words, for a short distance, we again see the combination ;48, and employ it by way of TERMINATION to what immediately precedes. We have thus this arrangement:

the tree ;4(4+?34 the,

or, substituting the natural letters, where known, it reads thus:

the tree thr+?3h the.

“Now, if, in place of the unknown characters, we leave blank spaces, or substitute dots, we read thus:

the tree thr...h the,

when the word 'through' makes itself evident at once. But this discovery gives us three new letters, o, u, and g, represented by +, ?, and 3.

"Looking now, narrowly, through the cipher for combinations of known characters, we find, not very far from the beginning, this arrangement,

83(88, or egree,

which plainly, is the conclusion of the word 'degree,' and gives us another letter, d, represented by !.

"Four letters beyond the word 'degree,' we perceive the combination

;46(;88.

"Translating the known characters, and representing the unknown by dots, as before, we read thus:

th.rtee,

an arrangement immediately suggestive of the word thirteen,' and again furnishing us with two new characters, i and n, represented by 6 and *.

"Referring, now, to the beginning of the cryptograph, we find the combination,

53++!.

"Translating as before, we obtain

good,

which assures us that the first letter is A, and that the first two words are ‘A good.’

“It is now time that we arrange our key, as far as discovered, in a tabular form, to avoid confusion. It will stand thus:

5 represents a<br>
! " d<br>
8 " e<br>
3 " g<br>
4 " h<br>
6 " i<br>
* " n<br>
+ " o<br>
( " r<br>
; " t<br>
? " u

“We have, therefore, no less than eleven of the most important letters represented, and it will be unnecessary to proceed with the details of the solution. I have said enough to convince you that ciphers of this nature are readily soluble, and to give you some insight into the rationale of their development. But be assured that the specimen before us appertains to the very simplest species of cryptograph. It now only remains to give you the full translation of the characters upon the parchment, as unriddled. Here it is:

> "A good glass in the bishop's hostel in the devil's seat forty-one degrees and thirteen minutes northeast and by north main branch seventh limb east side shoot from the left eye of the death's head a bee-line from the tree through the shot fifty feet out."

"But," said I, "the enigma seems still in as bad a condition as ever. How is it possible to extort a meaning from all this jargon about 'devil's seats,' 'death's heads,' and 'bishop's hostels'?"

"I confess," replied Legrand, "that the matter still wears a serious aspect, when regarded with a casual glance. My first endeavor was to divide the sentence into the natural division intended by the cryptographist."

"You mean, to punctuate it?"

"Something of that kind."

"But how was it possible to effect this?"

"I reflected that it had been a POINT with the writer to run his words together without division, so as to increase the difficulty of solution. Now, a not overacute man, in pursuing such an object, would be nearly certain to overdo the matter. When, in the course of his composition, he arrived at a break in his subject which would naturally require a pause, or a point, he would be exceedingly apt to run his characters, at this place, more than usually close together. If you will observe the MS., in the present instance, you will easily detect five such cases of unusual crowding. Acting upon this hint I made the division thus:

"'A good glass in the bishop's hostel in the devil's seat--forty- one degrees and thirteen minutes--northeast and by north--main branch seventh limb east side--shoot from the left eye of the death's head--a bee-line from the tree through the shot fifty feet out.'"

"Even this division," said I, "leaves me still in the dark."

"It left me also in the dark," replied Legrand, "for a few days; during which I made diligent inquiry in the neighborhood of Sullivan's Island, for any building which went by name of the "Bishop's Hotel'; for, of course, I dropped the obsolete word 'hostel.' Gaining no information on the subject, I was on the point of extending my sphere of search, and proceeding in a more systematic manner, when, one morning, it entered into my head, quite suddenly, that this 'Bishop's Hostel' might have some reference to an old family, of the name of Bessop, which, time out of mind, had held possession of an ancient manor house, about four miles to the northward of the island. I accordingly went over to the plantation, and reinstituted my inquiries among the older negroes of the place. At length one of the most aged of the women said that she had heard of such a place as Bessop's Castle, and thought that she could guide me to it, but that it was not a castle, nor a tavern, but a high rock.

"I offered to pay her well for her trouble, and, after some demur, she consented to accompany me to the spot. We found it without much difficulty, when, dismissing her, I proceeded to examine the place. The 'castle' consisted of an irregular assemblage of cliffs and rocks--one of the latter being quite remarkable for its height as well as for its insulated and artificial appearance. I clambered to its apex, and then felt much at a loss as to what should be next done.

"While I was busied in reflection, my eyes fell upon a narrow ledge in the eastern face of the rock, perhaps a yard below the summit upon which I stood. This ledge projected about eighteen inches, and was not more than a foot wide, while a niche in the cliff just above it gave it a rude resemblance to one of the hollow-backed chairs used by our ancestors. I made no doubt that here was the 'devil's seat' alluded to in the MS., and now I seemed to grasp the full secret of the riddle.

"The 'good glass,' I knew, could have reference to nothing but a telescope; for the word 'glass' is rarely employed in any other sense by seamen. Now here, I at once saw, was a telescope to be used, and a definite point of view, ADMITTING NO VARIATION, from which to use it. Nor did I hesitate to believe that the phrases, 'forty-one degrees and thirteen minutes,' and 'northeast and by north,' were intended as directions for the leveling of the glass. Greatly excited by these discoveries, I hurried home, procured a telescope, and returned to the rock.

"I let myself down to the ledge, and found that it was impossible to retain a seat upon it except in one particular position. This fact confirmed my preconceived idea. I proceeded to use the glass. Of course, the 'forty-one degrees and thirteen minutes' could allude to nothing but elevation above the visible horizon, since the horizontal direction was clearly indicated by the words, 'northeast and by north.' This latter direction I at once established by means of a pocket compass; then, pointing the glass as nearly at an angle of forty-one degrees of elevation as I could do it by guess, I moved it cautiously up or down, until my attention was arrested by a circular rift or opening in the foliage of a large tree that overtopped its fellows in the distance. In the center of this rift I perceived a white spot, but could not, at first, distinguish what it was. Adjusting the focus of the telescope, I again looked, and now made it out to be a human skull.

"Upon this discovery I was so sanguine as to consider the enigma solved; for the phrase 'main branch, seventh limb, east side,' could refer only to the position of the skull upon the tree, while 'shoot from the left eye of the death's head' admitted, also, of but one interpretation, in regard to a search for buried treasure. I perceived that the design was to drop a bullet from the left eye of the skull, and that a bee-line, or, in other words, a straight line, drawn from the nearest point of the trunk 'through the shot' (or the spot where the bullet fell), and thence extended to a distance of fifty feet, would indicate a definite point--and beneath this point I thought it at least POSSIBLE that a deposit of value lay concealed."

"All this," I said, "is exceedingly clear, and, although ingenious, still simple and explicit. When you left the Bishop's Hotel, what then?"

"Why, having carefully taken the bearings of the tree, I turned homeward. The instant that I left 'the devil's seat,' however, the circular rift vanished; nor could I get a glimpse of it afterwards, turn as I would. What seems to me the chief ingenuity in this whole business, is the fact (for repeated experiment has convinced me it IS a fact) that the circular opening in question is visible from no other attainable point of view than that afforded by the narrow ledge upon the face of the rock.

"In this expedition to the 'Bishop's Hotel' I had been attended by Jupiter, who had, no doubt, observed, for some weeks past, the abstraction of my demeanor, and took especial care not to leave me alone. But, on the next day, getting up very early, I contrived to give him the slip, and went into the hills in search of the tree. After much toil I found it. When I came home at night my valet proposed to give me a flogging. With the rest of the adventure I believe you are as well acquainted as myself."

"I suppose," said I, "you missed the spot, in the first attempt at digging, through Jupiter's stupidity in letting the bug fall through the right instead of through the left eye of the skull."

"Precisely. This mistake made a difference of about two inches and a half in the 'shot'--that is to say, in the position of the peg nearest the tree; and had the treasure been BENEATH the 'shot,' the error would have been of little moment; but 'the shot,' together with the nearest point of the tree, were merely two points for the establishment of a line of direction; of course the error, however trivial in the beginning, increased as we proceeded with the line, and by the time we had gone fifty feet threw us quite off the scent. But for my deep-seated impressions that treasure was here somewhere actually buried, we might have had all our labor in vain."

"But your grandiloquence, and your conduct in swinging the beetle-- how excessively odd! I was sure you were mad. And why did you insist upon letting fall the bug, instead of a bullet, from the skull?"

"Why, to be frank, I felt somewhat annoyed by your evident suspicions touching my sanity, and so resolved to punish you quietly, in my own way, by a little bit of sober mystification. For this reason I swung the beetle, and for this reason I let it fall from the tree. An observation of yours about its great weight suggested the latter idea."

"Yes, I perceive; and now there is only one point which puzzles me. What are we to make of the skeletons found in the hole?"

"That is a question I am no more able to answer than yourself. There seems, however, only one plausible way of accounting for them-- and yet it is dreadful to believe in such atrocity as my suggestion would imply. It is clear that Kidd--if Kidd indeed secreted this treasure, which I doubt not--it is clear that he must have had assistance in the labor. But this labor concluded, he may have thought it expedient to remove all participants in his secret. Perhaps a couple of blows with a mattock were sufficient, while his coadjutors were busy in the pit; perhaps it required a dozen--who shall tell?"

**THE END**

Edgar Allan Poe, medallion of bust, facing front.
*Courtesy of the Library of Congress*

# The Oblong Box
# 1844

Charleston harbor. *Courtesy of the Library of Congress.*

**"The death of a beautiful woman is unquestionably the most poetical topic in the world." – Edgar Allan Poe**

---

There is no doubt Poe's belief in "the most poetical topic in the world" was accurate. His tales are filled with beautiful women who die. At the time Poe wrote "The Oblong Box," his wife Virginia had been suffering the effects of tuberculosis for over two years. Her illness was already beginning to infect Poe's psyche. He was often despondent and began drinking heavily.

This story of grief and a descent into madness may have been an apt reflection of Poe's emotional state at the time. He obviously knew that his wife would never recover from the illness and he would soon have to deal with the reality of her death.

As if the pervasive atmosphere of madness, grief and despondency is not enough, Poe hints (slightly) at something unimaginably horrific – necrophilia.

# The Oblong Box

---

SOME YEARS AGO, I ENGAGED PASSAGE FROM Charleston, S. C, to the city of New York, in the fine packet-ship *Independence*, Captain Hardy. We were to sail on the fifteenth of the month (June), weather permitting; and on the fourteenth, I went on board to arrange some matters in my stateroom.

I found that we were to have a great many passengers, including a more than usual number of ladies. On the list were several of my acquaintances, and among other names, I was rejoiced to see that of Mr. Cornelius Wyatt, a young artist, for whom I entertained feelings of warm friendship. He had been with me a fellow-student at C---- University, where we were very much together. He had the ordinary temperament of genius, and was a compound of misanthropy, sensibility, and enthusiasm. To these qualities he united the warmest and truest heart which ever beat in a human bosom.

I observed that his name was carded upon THREE state-rooms; and, upon again referring to the list of passengers, I found that he had engaged passage for himself, wife, and two sisters--his own. The state-rooms were sufficiently roomy, and each had two berths, one above the other. These berths, to be sure, were so exceedingly narrow as to be insufficient for more than one person; still, I could not comprehend why there were THREE staterooms for these four persons. I was, just at that epoch, in one of those moody frames of mind which make a man abnormally inquisitive about trifles: and I confess, with shame, that I busied myself in a variety of ill- bred and preposterous conjectures about this matter of the supernumerary stateroom. It was no business of mine, to be sure, but with none the less pertinacity did I occupy myself in attempts to resolve the enigma. At last I reached a conclusion which wrought in me great wonder why I had not arrived at it before. "It is a servant of course," I said; "what a fool I am, not sooner to have thought of so obvious a solution!" And then I again repaired to the list--but here I saw distinctly that NO servant was to come with the party, although, in fact, it had been the original design to bring one--for the words "and servant" had been first written and then over-scored. "Oh, extra baggage, to be sure," I now said to myself—"something he wishes not to be put in the hold-- something to be kept under his own eye--ah, I have it--a painting or so--and this is what he has been bargaining about with Nicolino, the Italian Jew." This idea satisfied me, and I dismissed my curiosity for the nonce.

Wyatt's two sisters I knew very well, and most amiable and clever girls they were. His wife he had newly married, and I had never yet seen her. He had often talked about her in my presence, however, and in his usual style of enthusiasm. He described her as of surpassing beauty, wit, and accomplishment. I was, therefore, quite anxious to make her acquaintance.

On the day in which I visited the ship (the fourteenth), Wyatt and party were also to visit it--so the captain informed me--and I waited on board an hour longer than I had designed, in hope of being presented to the bride, but then an apology came. "Mrs. W. was a little indisposed, and would decline coming on board until to-morrow, at the hour of sailing."

The morrow having arrived, I was going from my hotel to the wharf, when Captain Hardy met me and said that, "owing to circumstances" (a stupid but convenient phrase), "he rather thought the *Independence* would not sail for a day or two, and that when all was ready, he would send up and let me know." This I thought strange, for there was a stiff southerly breeze; but as "the circumstances" were not forthcoming, although I pumped for them with much perseverance, I had nothing to do but to return home and digest my impatience at leisure.

I did not receive the expected message from the captain for nearly a week. It came at length, however, and I immediately went on board. The ship was crowded with passengers, and everything was in the bustle attendant upon making sail. Wyatt's party arrived in about ten minutes after myself. There were the two sisters, the bride, and the artist--the latter in one of his customary fits of moody misanthropy. I was too well used to these, however, to pay them any special attention. He did not even introduce me to his wife;--this courtesy devolving, per force, upon his sister Marian-- a very sweet and intelligent girl, who, in a few hurried words, made us acquainted.

Mrs. Wyatt had been closely veiled; and when she raised her veil, in acknowledging my bow, I confess that I was very profoundly astonished. I should have been much more so, however, had not long experience advised me not to trust, with too implicit a reliance, the enthusiastic descriptions of my friend, the artist, when indulging in comments upon the loveliness of woman. When beauty was the theme, I well knew with what facility he soared into the regions of the purely ideal.

The truth is, I could not help regarding Mrs. Wyatt as a decidedly plain-looking woman. If not positively ugly, she was not, I think, very far from it. She was dressed, however, in exquisite taste-- and then I had no doubt that she had captivated my friend's heart by the more enduring graces of the intellect and soul. She said very few words, and passed at once into her state-room with Mr. W.

My old inquisitiveness now returned. There was NO servant--THAT was a settled point. I looked, therefore, for the extra baggage. After some delay, a cart arrived at the wharf, with an oblong pine box, which was everything that seemed to be expected. Immediately upon its arrival we made sail, and in a short time were safely over the bar and standing out to sea.

The box in question was, as I say, oblong. It was about six feet in length by two and a half in breadth; I observed it attentively, and like to be precise. Now this shape was PECULIAR; and no sooner had I seen it, than I took credit to myself for the accuracy of my guessing. I had reached the conclusion, it will be remembered, that the extra baggage of my friend, the artist, would prove to be pictures, or at least a picture; for I knew he had been for several weeks in conference with Nicolino:--and now here was a box, which, from its shape, COULD possibly contain nothing in the world but a copy of Leonardo's "Last Supper;" and a copy of this very "Last Supper," done by Rubini the younger, at Florence, I had known, for some time, to be in the possession of Nicolino. This point, therefore, I considered as sufficiently settled. I chuckled excessively when I thought of my acumen. It was the first time I had ever known Wyatt to keep from me any of his artistical secrets; but here he evidently intended to steal a march upon me, and smuggle a fine picture to New York, under my very nose; expecting me to know nothing of the matter. I resolved to quiz him WELL, now and hereafter.

One thing, however, annoyed me not a little. The box did NOT go into the extra stateroom. It was deposited in Wyatt's own; and there, too, it remained, occupying very nearly the whole of the floor--no doubt to the exceeding discomfort of the artist and his wife;--this the more especially as the tar or paint with which it was lettered in sprawling capitals, emitted a strong, disagreeable, and, to my fancy, a peculiarly disgusting odor. On the lid were painted the words—"Mrs. Adelaide Curtis, Albany, New York. Charge of Cornelius Wyatt, Esq. This side up. To be handled with care."

Now, I was aware that Mrs. Adelaide Curtis, of Albany, was the artist's wife's mother,--but then I looked upon the whole address as a mystification, intended especially for myself. I made up my mind, of course, that the box and contents would never get farther north than the studio of my misanthropic friend, in Chambers Street, New York.

For the first three or four days we had fine weather, although the wind was dead ahead; having chopped round to the northward, immediately upon our losing sight of the coast. The passengers were, consequently, in high spirits and disposed to be social. I MUST except, however, Wyatt and his sisters, who behaved stiffly, and, I could not help thinking, uncourteously to the rest of the party. Wyatt's conduct I did not so much regard. He was gloomy, even beyond his usual habit--in fact he was MOROSE--but in him I was prepared for eccentricity. For the sisters, however, I could make no excuse. They secluded themselves in their staterooms during the greater part of the passage, and absolutely refused, although I repeatedly urged them, to hold communication with any person on board.

Mrs. Wyatt herself was far more agreeable. That is to say, she was CHATTY; and to be chatty is no slight recommendation at sea. She became EXCESSIVELY intimate with most of the ladies; and, to my profound astonishment, evinced no equivocal disposition to coquet with the men. She amused us all very much. I say "amused"--and scarcely know how to explain myself. The truth is, I soon found that Mrs. W. was far oftener laughed AT than WITH. The gentlemen said little about her; but the ladies, in a little while, pronounced her "a good-hearted thing, rather indifferent looking, totally uneducated, and decidedly vulgar." The great wonder was, how Wyatt had been entrapped into such a match. Wealth was the general solution--but this I knew to be no solution at all; for Wyatt had told me that she neither brought him a dollar nor had any expectations from any source whatever.

"He had married," he said, "for love, and for love only; and his bride was far more than worthy of his love." When I thought of these expressions, on the part of my friend, I confess that I felt indescribably puzzled. Could it be possible that he was taking leave of his senses? What else could I think? HE, so refined, so intellectual, so fastidious, with so exquisite a perception of the faulty, and so keen an appreciation of the beautiful! To be sure, the lady seemed especially fond of HIM--particularly so in his absence--when she made herself ridiculous by frequent quotations of what had been said by her "beloved husband, Mr. Wyatt." The word "husband" seemed forever--to use one of her own delicate expressions--forever "on the tip of her tongue." In the meantime, it was observed by all on board, that he avoided HER in the most pointed manner, and, for the most part, shut himself up alone in his state-room, where, in fact, he might have been said to live altogether, leaving his wife at full liberty to amuse herself as she thought best, in the public society of the main cabin.

My conclusion, from what I saw and heard, was, that, the artist, by some unaccountable freak of fate, or perhaps in some fit of enthusiastic and fanciful passion, had been induced to unite himself with a person altogether beneath him, and that the natural result, entire and speedy disgust, had ensued. I pitied him from the bottom of my heart--but could not, for that reason, quite forgive his incommunicativeness in the matter of the "Last Supper." For this I resolved to have my revenge.

One day he came upon deck, and, taking his arm as had been my wont, I sauntered with him backward and forward. His gloom, however (which I considered quite natural under the circumstances), seemed entirely unabated. He said little, and that moodily, and with evident effort. I ventured a jest or two, and he made a sickening attempt at a smile. Poor fellow!--as I thought of HIS WIFE, I wondered that he could have heart to put on even the semblance of mirth. At last I ventured a home thrust. I determined to commence a series of covert insinuations, or innuendoes, about the oblong box--just to let him perceive, gradually, that I was NOT altogether the butt, or victim, of his little bit of pleasant mystification. My first observation was by way of opening a masked battery. I said something about the "peculiar shape of THAT box--,"and, as I spoke the words, I smiled knowingly, winked, and touched him gently with my forefinger in the ribs.

The manner in which Wyatt received this harmless pleasantry convinced me, at once, that he was mad. At first he stared at me as if he found it impossible to comprehend the witticism of my remark; but as its point seemed slowly to make its way into his brain, his eyes, in the same proportion, seemed protruding from their sockets. Then he grew very red--then hideously pale--then, as if highly amused with what I had insinuated, he began a loud and boisterous laugh, which, to my astonishment, he kept up, with gradually increasing vigor, for ten minutes or more. In conclusion, he fell flat and heavily upon the deck. When I ran to uplift him, to all appearance he was DEAD.

I called assistance, and, with much difficulty, we brought him to himself. Upon reviving he spoke incoherently for some time. At length we bled him and put him to bed. The next morning he was quite recovered, so far as regarded his mere bodily health. Of his mind I say nothing, of course. I avoided him during the rest of the passage, by advice of the captain, who seemed to coincide with me altogether in my views of his insanity, but cautioned me to say nothing on this head to any person on board.

Several circumstances occurred immediately after this fit of Wyatt which contributed to heighten the curiosity with which I was already possessed. Among other things, this: I had been nervous-- drank too much strong green tea, and slept ill at night--in fact, for two nights I could not be properly said to sleep at all. Now, my state-room opened into the main cabin, or dining-room, as did those of all the single men on board. Wyatt's three rooms were in the after-cabin, which was separated from the main one by a slight sliding door, never locked even at night. As we were almost constantly on a wind, and the breeze was not a little stiff, the ship heeled to leeward very considerably; and whenever her starboard side was to leeward, the sliding door between the cabins slid open, and so remained, nobody taking the trouble to get up and shut it. But my berth was in such a position, that when my own state-room door was open, as well as the sliding door in question (and my own door was ALWAYS open on account of the heat,) I could see into the after-cabin quite distinctly, and just at that portion of it, too, where were situated the state-rooms of Mr. Wyatt. Well, during two nights (NOT consecutive) while I lay awake, I clearly saw Mrs. W., about eleven o'clock upon each night, steal cautiously from the state-room of Mr. W., and enter the extra room, where she remained until daybreak, when she was called by her husband and went back. That they were virtually separated was clear. They had separate apartments--no doubt in contemplation of a more permanent divorce; and here, after all I thought was the mystery of the extra stateroom.

There was another circumstance, too, which interested me much. During the two wakeful nights in question, and immediately after the disappearance of Mrs. Wyatt into the extra stateroom, I was attracted by certain singular cautious, subdued noises in that of her husband. After listening to them for some time, with thoughtful attention, I at length succeeded perfectly in translating their import. They were sounds occasioned by the artist in prying open the oblong box, by means of a chisel and mallet--the latter being apparently muffled, or deadened, by some soft woollen or cotton substance in which its head was enveloped.

In this manner I fancied I could distinguish the precise moment when he fairly disengaged the lid--also, that I could determine when he removed it altogether, and when he deposited it upon the lower berth in his room; this latter point I knew, for example, by certain slight taps which the lid made in striking against the wooden edges of the berth, as he endeavored to lay it down VERY gently--there being no room for it on the floor. After this there was a dead stillness, and I heard nothing more, upon either occasion, until nearly daybreak; unless, perhaps, I may mention a low sobbing, or murmuring sound, so very much suppressed as to be nearly inaudible--if, indeed, the whole of this latter noise were not rather produced by my own imagination. I say it seemed to RESEMBLE sobbing or sighing--but, of course, it could not have been either. I rather think it was a ringing in my own ears. Mr. Wyatt, no doubt, according to custom, was merely giving the rein to one of his hobbies--indulging in one of his fits of artistic enthusiasm. He had opened his oblong box, in order to feast his eyes on the pictorial treasure within. There was nothing in this, however, to make him SOB. I repeat, therefore, that it must have been simply a freak of my own fancy, distempered by good Captain Hardy's green tea. just before dawn, on each of the two nights of which I speak, I distinctly heard Mr. Wyatt replace the lid upon the oblong box, and force the nails into their old places by means of the muffled mallet. Having done this, he issued from his state- room, fully dressed, and proceeded to call Mrs. W. from hers.

We had been at sea seven days, and were now off Cape Hatteras, when there came a tremendously heavy blow from the southwest. We were, in a measure, prepared for it, however, as the weather had been holding out threats for some time. Everything was made snug, alow and aloft; and as the wind steadily freshened, we lay to, at length, under spanker and foretopsail, both double-reefed.

In this trim we rode safely enough for forty-eight hours--the ship proving herself an excellent sea-boat in many respects, and shipping no water of any consequence. At the end of this period, however, the gale had freshened into a hurricane, and our after-- sail split into ribbons, bringing us so much in the trough of the water that we shipped several prodigious seas, one immediately after the other. By this accident we lost three men overboard with the caboose, and nearly the whole of the larboard bulwarks. Scarcely had we recovered our senses, before the foretopsail went into shreds, when we got up a storm staysail and with this did pretty well for some hours, the ship heading the sea much more steadily than before.

The gale still held on, however, and we saw no signs of its abating. The rigging was found to be ill-fitted, and greatly strained; and on the third day of the blow, about five in the afternoon, our mizzen-mast, in a heavy lurch to windward, went by the board. For an hour or more, we tried in vain to get rid of it, on account of the prodigious rolling of the ship; and, before we had succeeded, the carpenter came aft and announced four feet of water in the hold. To add to our dilemma, we found the pumps choked and nearly useless.

All was now confusion and despair--but an effort was made to lighten the ship by throwing overboard as much of her cargo as could be reached, and by cutting away the two masts that remained. This we at last accomplished--but we were still unable to do anything at the pumps; and, in the meantime, the leak gained on us very fast.

At sundown, the gale had sensibly diminished in violence, and as the sea went down with it, we still entertained faint hopes of saving ourselves in the boats. At eight P. M., the clouds broke away to windward, and we had the advantage of a full moon--a piece of good fortune which served wonderfully to cheer our drooping spirits.

After incredible labor we succeeded, at length, in getting the longboat over the side without material accident, and into this we crowded the whole of the crew and most of the passengers. This party made off immediately, and, after undergoing much suffering, finally arrived, in safety, at Ocracoke Inlet, on the third day after the wreck.

Fourteen passengers, with the captain, remained on board, resolving to trust their fortunes to the jolly-boat at the stern. We lowered it without difficulty, although it was only by a miracle that we prevented it from swamping as it touched the water. It contained, when afloat, the captain and his wife, Mr. Wyatt and party, a Mexican officer, wife, four children, and myself, with a negro valet.

We had no room, of course, for anything except a few positively necessary instruments, some provisions, and the clothes upon our backs. No one had thought of even attempting to save anything more. What must have been the astonishment of all, then, when having proceeded a few fathoms from the ship, Mr. Wyatt stood up in the stern-sheets, and coolly demanded of Captain Hardy that the boat should be put back for the purpose of taking in his oblong box!

"Sit down, Mr. Wyatt," replied the captain, somewhat sternly, "you will capsize us if you do not sit quite still. Our gunwhale is almost in the water now."

"The box!" vociferated Mr. Wyatt, still standing—"the box, I say! Captain Hardy, you cannot, you will not refuse me. Its weight will be but a trifle--it is nothing--mere nothing. By the mother who bore you--for the love of Heaven--by your hope of salvation, I implore you to put back for the box!"

The captain, for a moment, seemed touched by the earnest appeal of the artist, but he regained his stern composure, and merely said:

"Mr. Wyatt, you are mad. I cannot listen to you. Sit down, I say, or you will swamp the boat. Stay--hold him--seize him!--he is about to spring overboard! There--I knew it--he is over!"

As the captain said this, Mr. Wyatt, in fact, sprang from the boat, and, as we were yet in the lee of the wreck, succeeded, by almost superhuman exertion, in getting hold of a rope which hung from the fore-chains. In another moment he was on board, and rushing frantically down into the cabin.

In the meantime, we had been swept astern of the ship, and being quite out of her lee, were at the mercy of the tremendous sea which was still running. We made a determined effort to put back, but our little boat was like a feather in the breath of the tempest. We saw at a glance that the doom of the unfortunate artist was sealed.

As our distance from the wreck rapidly increased, the madman (for as such only could we regard him) was seen to emerge from the companion--way, up which by dint of strength that appeared gigantic, he dragged, bodily, the oblong box. While we gazed in the extremity of astonishment, he passed, rapidly, several turns of a three-inch rope, first around the box and then around his body. In another instant both body and box were in the sea--disappearing suddenly, at once and forever.

We lingered awhile sadly upon our oars, with our eyes riveted upon the spot. At length we pulled away. The silence remained unbroken for an hour. Finally, I hazarded a remark.

"Did you observe, captain, how suddenly they sank? Was not that an exceedingly singular thing? I confess that I entertained some feeble hope of his final deliverance, when I saw him lash himself to the box, and commit himself to the sea."

"They sank as a matter of course," replied the captain, "and that like a shot. They will soon rise again, however--BUT NOT TILL THE SALT MELTS."

"The salt!" I ejaculated.

"Hush!" said the captain, pointing to the wife and sisters of the deceased. "We must talk of these things at some more appropriate time."

We suffered much, and made a narrow escape, but fortune befriended us, as well as our mates in the long-boat. We landed, in fine, more dead than alive, after four days of intense distress, upon the beach opposite Roanoke Island. We remained here a week, were not ill-treated by the wreckers, and at length obtained a passage to New York.

About a month after the loss of the *Independence,* I happened to meet Captain Hardy in Broadway. Our conversation turned, naturally, upon the disaster, and especially upon the sad fate of poor Wyatt. I thus learned the following particulars.

The artist had engaged passage for himself, wife, two sisters and a servant. His wife was, indeed, as she had been represented, a most lovely, and most accomplished woman. On the morning of the fourteenth of June (the day in which I first visited the ship), the lady suddenly sickened and died. The young husband was frantic with grief--but circumstances imperatively forbade the deferring his voyage to New York. It was necessary to take to her mother the corpse of his adored wife, and, on the other hand, the universal prejudice which would prevent his doing so openly was well known. Nine-tenths of the passengers would have abandoned the ship rather than take passage with a dead body.

In this dilemma, Captain Hardy arranged that the corpse, being first partially embalmed, and packed, with a large quantity of salt, in a box of suitable dimensions, should be conveyed on board as merchandise. Nothing was to be said of the lady's decease; and, as it was well understood that Mr. Wyatt had engaged passage for his wife, it became necessary that some person should personate her during the voyage. This the deceased lady's-maid was easily prevailed on to do. The extra state-room, originally engaged for this girl during her mistress' life, was now merely retained. In this state-room the pseudo-wife, slept, of course, every night. In the daytime she performed, to the best of her ability, the part of her mistress--whose person, it had been carefully ascertained, was unknown to any of the passengers on board.

My own mistake arose, naturally enough, through too careless, too inquisitive, and too impulsive a temperament. But of late, it is a rare thing that I sleep soundly at night. There is a countenance which haunts me, turn as I will. There is an hysterical laugh which will forever ring within my ears.

**THE END**

# The Balloon-Hoax
# 1844

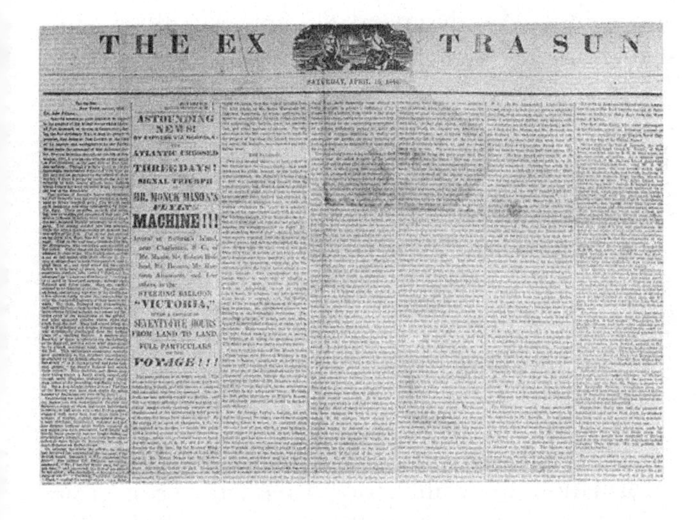

THE EXTRA SUN

ASTOUNDING NEWS!

ATLANTIC CROSSED

THREE DAYS!

SIGNAL TRIUMPH

MR. MONCK MASON'S

FLYING

MACHINE!!!

"VICTORIA,"

SEVENTY-FIVE HOURS

FROM LAND TO LAND

FULL PARTICULARS

VOYAGE!!!

Original front page of The New York Sun which published "The Balloon-Hoax." *Public Domain*

**"Science has not yet taught us if madness is or is not the sublimity of the intelligence."**

**– Edgar Allan Poe**

---

Written as it were a real piece of journalism, this story created a sensation when published and could be described as early science fiction, as well as being a grand entry of the long tradition of literary hoaxes and games. Poe described the enthusiasm his story had aroused.

"I never witnessed more intense excitement to get possession of a newspaper," he wrote. "The *Sun* building was besieged."

Poe added realistic elements, discussing at length the balloon's design and propulsion system in believable detail. His use of real people, including William Harrison Ainsworth, also lent credence to the story.

Due to intense public interest for more information about the story, a retraction concerning the article was printed in *The Sun* on April 15, 1844:

> BALLOON - The mails from the South last Saturday night not having brought a confirmation of the arrival of the Balloon from England, the particulars of which from our correspondent we detailed in our Extra, we are inclined to believe that the intelligence is erroneous. The description of the Balloon and

the voyage was written with a minuteness and scientific ability calculated to obtain credit everywhere, and was read with great pleasure and satisfaction. We by no means think such a project impossible.

# THE BALLOON-HOAX

---

*Sun* Office, April 12, 10 o□clock A.M.
**ASTOUNDING NEWS BY EXPRESS, VIA NORFOLK!**
The Atlantic Crossed in Three Days!
Signal Triumph of Mr. Monck Mason□s Flying Machine!
Arrival at Sullivan□s Island, near Charlestown, S. C., of Mr. Mason, Mr. Robert Holland, Mr. Henson, Mr. Harrison Ainsworth, and four others, in the Steering Balloon, Victoria, after a Passage of Seventy-five Hours from Land to Land!
**Full Particulars of the Voyage!**

*The subjoined jeu d'esprit with the preceding heading in magnificent capitals, well interspersed with notes of admiration, was originally published, as matter of fact, in the New York Sun, a daily newspaper, and therein fully subserved the purpose of creating indigestible aliment for the quidnuncs during the few hours intervening between a couple of the Charleston mails. The rush for the "sole paper which had the news" was something beyond even the prodigious; and, in fact, if (as some assert) the Victoria did not absolutely accomplish the voyage recorded it will be difficult to assign a reason why she should not have accomplished it. E. A. P.*

THE GREAT PROBLEM IS AT LENGTH SOLVED! THE air, as well as the earth and the ocean, has been subdued by science, and will become a common and convenient highway for mankind. The Atlantic has been actually crossed in a Balloon! and this too without difficulty-without any great apparent danger-with thorough control of the machine-and in the inconceivably brief period of seventy-five hours from shore to shore! By the energy of an agent at Charleston, S. C., we are enabled to be the first to furnish the public with a detailed account of this most extraordinary voyage, which was performed between Saturday, the 6th instant, at 11 A.M. and 2 P.M., on Tuesday, the 9th instant, by Sir Everard Bringhurst; Mr. Osborne, a nephew of Lord Bentinck's; Mr. Monck Mason and Mr. Robert Holland, the well-known aeronauts; Mr. Harrison Ainsworth, author of "Jack Sheppard,""etc.; and Mr. Henson the projector of the late unsuccessful flying machine-with two seamen from Woolwich-in all, eight persons. The particulars furnished below may be relied on as authentic and accurate in every respect, as, with a slight exception, they are copied verbatim from the joint diaries of Mr. Monck Mason and Mr. Harrison Ainsworth, to whose politeness our agent is also indebted for much verbal information respecting the balloon itself, its construction, and other matters of interest. The only alteration in the MS. received, has been made for the purpose of throwing the hurried account of our agent, Mr. Forsyth, into a connected and intelligible form.

## THE BALLOON

Two very decided failures, of late,-those of Mr. Henson and Sir George Cayley,-had much weakened the public interest in the subject of aerial navigation. Mr. Henson's scheme (which at first was considered very feasible even by men of science) was founded upon the principle of an inclined plane, started from an eminence by an extrinsic force, applied and continued by the revolution of impinging vanes, in form and number resembling the vanes of a windmill. But, in all the experiments made with models at the Adelaide Gallery, it was found that the operation of these fins not only did not propel the machine, but actually impeded its flight. The only propelling force it ever exhibited, was the mere impetus acquired from the descent of the inclined plane, and this impetus carried the machine farther when the vanes were at rest, than when they were in motion-a fact which sufficiently demonstrates their inutility, and in the absence of the propelling, which was also the sustaining power, the whole fabric would necessarily descend. This consideration led Sir George Cayley to think only of adapting a propeller to some machine having of itself an independent power of support-in a word, to a balloon; the idea, however, being novel, or original, with Sir George, only so far as regards the mode of its application to practice. He exhibited a model of his invention at the Polytechnic Institution. The propelling principle, or power, was here, also, applied to interrupted surfaces, or vanes, put in revolution. These vanes were four in number, but were found entirely ineffectual in moving the balloon, or in aiding its ascending power. The whole project was thus a complete failure.

It was at this juncture that Mr. Monck Mason (whose voyage from Dover to Weilburg in the balloon Nassau occasioned so much excitement in 1837) conceived the idea of employing the principle of the Archimedean screw for the purpose of propulsion through the air- rightly attributing the failure of Mr. Henson's scheme, and of Sir George Cayley's to the interruption of surface in the independent vanes. He made the first public experiment at Willis's Rooms, but afterward removed his model to the Adelaide Gallery.

Like Sir George Cayley's balloon, his own was an ellipsoid. Its length was 13 feet 6 inches-height, 6 feet 8 inches. It contained about 320 cubic feet of gas, which, if pure hydrogen, would support 21 pounds upon its first inflation, before the gas has time to deteriorate or escape. The weight of the whole machine and apparatus was 17 pounds-leaving about 4 pounds to spare. Beneath the centre of the balloon, was a frame of light wood, about 9 feet long, and rigged on to the balloon itself with a net-work in the customary manner. From this framework was suspended a wicker basket or car.

The screw consists of an axis of hollow brass tube, 18 inches in length, through which, upon a semi-spiral inclined at 15 degrees, pass a series of steel-wire radii, 2 feet long, and thus projecting a foot on either side. These radii are connected at the outer extremities by 2 bands of flattened wire; the whole in this manner forming the framework of the screw, which is completed by a covering of oiled silk cut into gores, and tightened so as to present a tolerably uniform surface. At each end of its axis this screw is supported by pillars of hollow brass tube descending from the hoop. In the lower ends of these tubes are holes in which the pivots of the axis revolve. From the end of the axis which is next the car, proceeds a shaft of steel, connecting the screw with the pinion of a piece of spring machinery fixed in the car. By the operation of this spring, the screw is made to revolve with great rapidity, communicating a progressive motion to the whole. By means of the rudder, the machine was readily turned in any direction. The spring was of great power, compared with its dimensions, being capable of raising 45 pounds upon a barrel of 4 inches diameter, after the first turn, and gradually increasing as it was wound up. It weighed, altogether, eight pounds six ounces. The rudder was a light frame of cane covered with silk, shaped somewhat like a battledoor, and was about 3 feet long, and at the widest, one foot. Its weight was about 2 ounces. It could be turned flat, and directed upward or downward, as well as to the right or left-, and thus enabled the aeronaut to transfer the resistance of the air which in an inclined position it must generate in its passage, to any side upon which he might desire to act; thus determining the balloon in the opposite direction.

This model (which, through want of time, we have necessarily described in an imperfect manner) was put in action at the Adelaide Gallery, where it accomplished a velocity of 5 miles per hour; although, strange to say, it excited very little interest in comparison with the previous complex machine of Mr. Henson-so resolute is the world to despise anything which carries with it an air of simplicity. To accomplish the great desideratum of aerial navigation, it was very generally supposed that some exceedingly complicated application must be made of some unusually profound principle in dynamics.

So well satisfied, however, was Mr. Mason of the ultimate success of his invention, that he determined to construct immediately, if possible, a balloon of sufficient capacity to test the question by a voyage of some extent; the original design being to cross the British Channel, as before, in the Nassau balloon. To carry out his views, he solicited and obtained the patronage of Sir Everard Bringhurst and Mr. Osborne, two gentlemen well known for scientific acquirement, and especially for the interest they have exhibited in the progress of aerostation.

The project, at the desire of Mr. Osborne, was kept a profound secret from the public-the only persons entrusted with the design being those actually engaged in the construction of the machine, which was built (under the superintendence of Mr. Mason, Mr. Holland, Sir Everard Bringhurst, and Mr. Osborne) at the seat of the latter gentleman near Penstruthal, in Wales. Mr. Henson, accompanied by his friend Mr. Ainsworth, was admitted to a private view of the balloon, on Saturday last; when the two gentlemen made final arrangements to be included in the adventure. We are not informed for what reason the two seamen were also included in the party-but in the course of a day or two, we shall put our readers in possession of the minutest particulars respecting this extraordinary voyage.

The balloon is composed of silk, varnished with the liquid gum caoutchouc. It is of vast dimensions, containing more than 40,000 cubic feet of gas; but as coal gas was employed in place of the more expensive and inconvenient hydrogen, the supporting power of the machine, when fully inflated, and immediately after inflation, is not more than about 2500 pounds. The coal gas is not only much less costly, but is easily procured and managed.

For its introduction into common use for purposes of aerostation, we are indebted to Mr. Charles Green. Up to his discovery, the process of inflation was not only exceedingly expensive, but uncertain. Two and even three days have frequently been wasted in futile attempts to procure a sufficiency of hydrogen to fill a balloon, from which it had great tendency to escape, owing to its extreme subtlety, and its affinity for the surrounding atmosphere. In a balloon sufficiently perfect to retain its contents of coal gas unaltered, in quantity or amount, for six months, an equal quantity of hydrogen could not be maintained in equal purity for six weeks.

The supporting power being estimated at 2500 pounds, and the united weights of the party amounting only to about 1200, there was left a surplus of 1300, of which again 1200 was exhausted by ballast, arranged in bags of different sizes, with their respective weights marked upon them-by cordage, barometers, telescopes, barrels containing provision for a fortnight, water-casks, cloaks, carpet-bags, and various other indispensable matters, including a coffee-warmer, contrived for warming coffee by means of slack-lime, so as to dispense altogether with fire, if it should be judged prudent to do so. All these articles, with the exception of the ballast, and a few trifles, were suspended from the hoop overhead. The car is much smaller and lighter, in proportion, than the one appended to the model. It is formed of a light wicker, and is wonderfully strong for so frail looking a machine. Its rim is about 4 feet deep. The rudder is also very much larger, in proportion, than that of the model; and the screw is considerably smaller. The balloon is furnished besides with a grapnel, and a guide-rope, which latter is of the most indispensable importance. A few words, in explanation, will here be necessary for such of our readers as are not conversant with the details of aerostation.

As soon as the balloon quits the earth, it is subjected to the influence of many circumstances tending to create a difference in its weight; augmenting or diminishing its ascending power. For example, there may be a deposition of dew upon the silk, to the extent, even, of several hundred pounds; ballast has then to be thrown out, or the machine may descend. This ballast being discarded, and a clear sunshine evaporating the dew, and at the same time expanding the gas in the silk, the whole will again rapidly ascend. To check this ascent, the only recourse is (or rather was, until Mr. Green"s invention of the guide-rope) the permission of the escape of gas from the valve; but, in the loss of gas, is a proportionate general loss of ascending power; so that, in a comparatively brief period, the best-constructed balloon must necessarily exhaust all its resources, and come to the earth. This was the great obstacle to voyages of length.

The guide-rope remedies the difficulty in the simplest manner conceivable. It is merely a very long rope which is suffered to trail from the car, and the effect of which is to prevent the balloon from changing its level in any material degree. If, for example, there should be a deposition of moisture upon, the silk, and the machine begins to descend in consequence, there will be no necessity for discharging ballast to remedy the increase of weight, for it is remedied, or counteracted, in an exactly just proportion, by the deposit on the ground of just so much of the end of the rope as is necessary. If, on the other hand, any circumstances should cause undue levity, and consequent ascent, this levity is immediately counteracted by the additional weight of rope upraised from the earth. Thus, the balloon can neither ascend nor descend, except within very narrow limits, and its resources, either in gas or ballast, remain comparatively unimpaired. When passing over an expanse of water, it becomes necessary to employ small kegs of copper or wood, filled with liquid ballast of a lighter nature than water. These float, and serve all the purposes of a mere rope on land.

Another most important office of the guide-rope, is to point out the direction of the balloon. The rope drags, either on land or sea, while the balloon is free; the latter, consequently, is always in advance, when any progress whatever is made, a comparison, therefore, by means of the compass, of the relative positions of the two objects, will always indicate the course. In the same way, the angle formed by the rope with the vertical axis of the machine, indicates the velocity. When there is no angle-in other words, when the rope hangs perpendicularly, the whole apparatus is stationary; but the larger the angle, that is to say, the farther the balloon precedes the end of the rope, the greater the velocity; and the converse.

As the original design was to cross the British Channel, and alight as near Paris as possible, the voyagers had taken the precaution to prepare themselves with passports directed to all parts of the Continent, specifying the nature of the expedition, as in the case of the Nassau voyage, and entitling the adventurers to exemption from the usual formalities of office; unexpected events, however, rendered these passports superfluous.

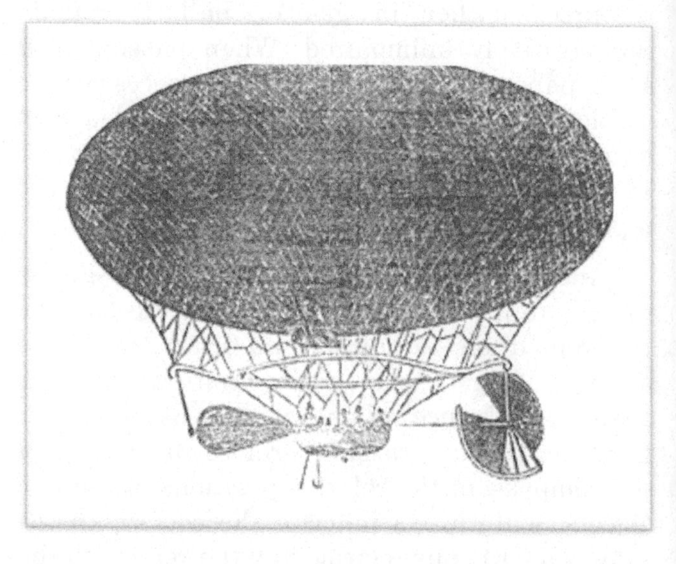

**Illustration from the original publication of "The Balloon-Hoax, Saturday, April 13, 1844, issue of the *New York Sun. Public Domain.***

The inflation was commenced very quietly at day-break, on Saturday morning, the 6th instant in the courtyard of Wheal-Vor House, Mr.

Osborne's seat, about a mile from Penstruthal, in North Wales; and at 7 minutes past 11, everything being ready for departure, the balloon was set free, rising gently but steadily, in a direction nearly South; no use being made, for the first half hour, of either the screw or the rudder. We proceed now with the journal, as transcribed by Mr. Forsyth from the joint MSS. of Mr. Monck Mason and Mr. Ainsworth. The body of the journal, as given, is in the handwriting of Mr. Mason, and a P. S. is appended, each day, by Mr. Ainsworth, who has in preparation, and will shortly give the public a more minute and, no doubt, a thrillingly interesting account of the voyage.

## THE JOURNAL

### Saturday, April the 6th.

Every preparation likely to embarrass us having been made overnight, we commenced the inflation this morning at daybreak; but owing to a thick fog which encumbered the folds of the silk and rendered it unmanageable, we did not get through before nearly eleven o'clock. Cut loose, then, in high spirits, and rose gently but steadily, with a light breeze at North, which bore us in the direction of the Bristol Channel. Found the ascending force greater than we had expected; and as we arose higher and so got clear of the cliffs, and more in the sun's rays, our ascent became very rapid. I did not wish, however, to lose gas at so early a period of the adventure, and so concluded to ascend for the present. We soon ran out our guide-rope; but even when we had raised it clear of the earth, we still went up very rapidly. The balloon was unusually steady, and looked beautifully. In about 10 minutes after starting, the barometer indicated an altitude of 15,000 feet. The weather was remarkably fine, and the view of the subjacent country-a most romantic one when seen from any point-was now especially sublime. The numerous deep gorges presented the appearance of lakes, on account of the dense vapors with which they were filled, and the pinnacles and crags to the South East, piled in inextricable confusion, resembling nothing so much as the giant cities of Eastern fable. We were rapidly approaching the mountains in the South, but our elevation was more than sufficient to enable us to pass them in safety.

In a few minutes we soared over them in fine style; and Mr. Ainsworth, with the seamen, was surprised at their apparent want of altitude when viewed from the car, the tendency of great elevation in a balloon being to reduce inequalities of the surface below, to nearly a dead level. At half-past eleven still proceeding nearly South, we obtained our first view of the Bristol Channel; and, in fifteen minutes afterward, the line of breakers on the coast appeared immediately beneath us, and we were fairly out at sea. We now resolved to let off enough gas to bring our guide-rope, with the buoys affixed, into the water. This was immediately done, and we commenced a gradual descent.

In about 20 minutes our first buoy dipped, and at the touch of the second soon afterward, we remained stationary as to elevation. We were all now anxious to test the efficiency of the rudder and screw, and we put them both into requisition forthwith, for the purpose of altering our direction more to the eastward, and in a line for Paris.

By means of the rudder we instantly effected the necessary change of direction, and our course was brought nearly at right angles to that of the wind; when we set in motion the spring of the screw, and were rejoiced to find it propel us readily as desired. Upon this we gave nine hearty cheers, and dropped in the sea a bottle, inclosing a slip of parchment with a brief account of the principle of the invention. Hardly, however, had we done with our rejoicings, when an unforeseen accident occurred which discouraged us in no little degree. The steel rod connecting the spring with the propeller was suddenly jerked out of place, at the car end, (by a swaying of the car through some movement of one of the two seamen we had taken up,) and in an instant hung dangling out of reach, from the pivot of the axis of the screw. While we were endeavoring to regain it, our attention being completely absorbed, we became involved in a strong current of wind from the East, which bore us, with rapidly increasing force, toward the Atlantic. We soon found ourselves driving out to sea at the rate of not less, certainly, than 50 or 60 miles an hour, so that we came up with Cape Clear, at some 40 miles to our North, before we had secured the rod, and had time to think what we were about.

It was now that Mr. Ainsworth made an extraordinary but, to my fancy, a by no means unreasonable or chimerical proposition, in which he was instantly seconded by Mr. Holland-viz.: that we should take advantage of the strong gale which bore us on, and in place of beating back to Paris, make an attempt to reach the coast of North America. After slight reflection, I gave a willing assent to this bold proposition, which (strange to say) met with objection from the two seamen only. As the stronger party, however, we overruled their fears, and kept resolutely upon our course.

We steered due West; but as the trailing of the buoys materially impeded our progress, and we had the balloon abundantly at command, either for ascent or descent, we first threw out fifty pounds of ballast, and then wound up (by means of a windlass) so much of the rope as brought it quite clear of the sea. We perceived the effect of this manoeuvre immediately, in a vastly increased rate of progress; and, as the gale freshened, we flew with a velocity nearly inconceivable; the guide-rope flying out behind the car, like a streamer from a vessel. It is needless to say that a very short time sufficed us to lose sight of the coast. We passed over innumerable vessels of all kinds, a few of which were endeavoring to beat up, but the most of them lying to. We occasioned the greatest excitement on board all-an excitement greatly relished by ourselves, and especially by our two men, who, now under the influence of a dram of Geneva, seemed resolved to give all scruple, or fear, to the wind. Many of the vessels fired signal guns; and in all we were saluted with loud cheers (which we heard with surprising distinctness) and the waving of caps and handkerchiefs. We kept on in this manner throughout the day with no material incident, and, as the shades of night closed around us, we made a rough estimate of the distance traversed. It could not have been less than 500 miles, and was probably much more. The propeller was kept in constant operation, and, no doubt, aided our progress materially. As the sun went down, the gale freshened into an absolute hurricane, and the ocean beneath was clearly visible on account of its phosphorescence. The wind was from the East all night, and gave us the brightest omen of success. We suffered no little from cold, and the dampness of the atmosphere was most unpleasant; but the ample space in the car enabled us to lie down, and by means of cloaks and a few blankets we did sufficiently well.

**P.S.** *[by Mr. Ainsworth.]*

The last nine hours have been unquestionably the most exciting of my life. I can conceive nothing more sublimating than the strange peril and novelty of an adventure such as this. May God grant that we succeed! I ask not success for mere safety to my insignificant person, but for the sake of human knowledge and-for the vastness of the triumph. And yet the feat is only so evidently feasible that the sole wonder is why men have scrupled to attempt it before. One single gale such as now befriends us-let such a tempest whirl forward a balloon for 4 or 5 days (these gales often last longer) and the voyager will be easily borne, in that period, from coast to coast. In view of such a gale the broad Atlantic becomes a mere lake. I am more struck, just now, with the supreme silence which reigns in the sea beneath us, notwithstanding its agitation, than with any other phenomenon presenting itself. The waters give up no voice to the Heavens. The immense flaming ocean writhes and is tortured uncomplainingly. The mountainous surges suggest the idea of innumerable dumb gigantic fiends struggling in impotent agony. In a night such as is this to me, a man lives-lives a whole century of ordinary life-nor would I forego this rapturous delight for that of a whole century of ordinary existence.

**Sunday, the 7th.** *[Mr. Mason's MS.]*

This morning the gale, by 10, had subsided to an eight- or nine-knot breeze (for a vessel at sea), and bears us, perhaps, 30 miles per hour, or more. It has veered, however, very considerably to the North; and now, at sundown, we are holding our course due West, principally by the screw and rudder, which answer their purposes to admiration. I regard the project as thoroughly successful, and the easy navigation of the air in any direction (not exactly in the teeth of a gale) as no longer problematical. We could not have made head against the strong wind of yesterday, but, by ascending, we might have got out of its influence, if requisite. Against a pretty stiff breeze, I feel convinced, we can make our way with the propeller. At noon, today, ascended to an elevation of nearly 25,000 feet, (about the height of Cotopaxi) by discharging ballast. Did this to search for a more direct current, but found none so favorable as the one we are now in. We have an abundance of gas to take us across this small pond, even should the voyage last 3 weeks. I have not the slightest fear for the result. The difficulty has been strangely exaggerated and misapprehended. I can choose my current, and should I find all currents against me, I can make very tolerable headway with the propeller. We have had no incidents worth recording. The night promises fair.

P.S. *[By Mr. Ainsworth.]*

I have little to record, except the fact (to me quite a surprising one) that, at an elevation equal to that of Cotopaxi, I experienced neither very intense cold, nor headache, nor difficulty of breathing; neither, I find, did Mr. Mason, nor Mr. Holland, nor Sir Everard. Mr. Osborne complained of constriction of the chest-but this soon wore off. We have flown at a great rate during the day, and we must be more than half way across the Atlantic. We have passed over some 20 or 30 vessels of various kinds, and all seem to be delightfully astonished. Crossing the ocean in a balloon is not so difficult a feat after all. Omne ignotum pro magnifico. Mem.: at 25,000 feet elevation the sky appears nearly black, and the stars are distinctly visible; while the sea does not seem convex (as one might suppose) but absolutely and most unequivocally concave.*

* "Mr. Ainsworth has not attempted to account for this phenomenon, which however, is quite susceptible of explanation. A line dropped from an elevation of 25,000 feet, perpendicularly to the surface of the earth (or sea), would form the perpendicular of a right-angled triangle, of which the base would extend from the right angle to the horizon, and the hypothenuse from the horizon to the balloon. But the 25,000 feet of altitude is little or nothing, in comparison with the extent of the prospect. In other words, the base and hypothenuse of the supposed triangle would be so long, when compared with the perpendicular, that the two former may be regarded as nearly parallel. In this manner the horizon of the aeronaut would appear to be on a level with the car. But, as the point immediately beneath him seems, and is, at a great distance below him, it seems, of course, also, at a great distance below the horizon. Hence the impression of concavity; and this impression must remain, until the elevation shall bear so great a proportion to the extent of prospect, that the apparent parallelism of the base and hypothenuse

disappears-when the earth's real convexity must appear.

**Monday, the 8th.** *[Mr. Mason's MS.]*

This morning we had again some little trouble with the rod of the propeller, which must be entirely remodelled, for fear of serious accident-I mean the steel rod, not the vanes. The latter could not be improved. The wind has been blowing steadily and strongly from the North-East all day; and so far fortune seems bent upon favoring us. Just before day, we were all somewhat alarmed at some odd noises and concussions in the balloon, accompanied with the apparent rapid subsidence of the whole machine. These phenomena were occasioned by the expansion of the gas, through increase of heat in the atmosphere, and the consequent disruption of the minute particles of ice with which the network had become encrusted during the night. Threw down several bottles to the vessels below. Saw one of them picked up by a large ship-seemingly one of the New York line packets. Endeavored to make out her name, but could not be sure of it. Mr. Osbornes telescope made it out something like "Atalanta." It is now 12 at night, and we are still going nearly West, at a rapid pace. The sea is peculiarly phosphorescent.

**P.S.** *[By Mr. Ainsworth.]*

It is now 2 A.M., and nearly calm, as well as I can judge-but it is very difficult to determine this point since we move with the air so completely. I have not slept since quitting Wheal-Vor, but can stand it no longer, and must take a nap. We cannot be far from the American coast.

**Tuesday, the 9th.** *[Mr. Ainsworth's MS.]* **One, P.M.**

We are in full view of the low coast of South Carolina. The great problem is accomplished. We have crossed the Atlantic-fairly and easily crossed it in a balloon! God be praised! Who shall say that anything is impossible hereafter?

The Journal here ceases. Some particulars of the descent were communicated, however, by Mr. Ainsworth to Mr. Forsyth. It was nearly dead calm when the voyagers first came in view of the coast, which was immediately recognized by both the seamen, and by Mr. Osborne. The latter gentleman having acquaintances at Fort Moultrie, it was immediately resolved to descend in its vicinity. The balloon was brought over the beach (the tide being out and the sand hard, smooth, and admirably adapted for a descent), and the grapnel let go, which took firm hold at once. The inhabitants of the Island, and of the Fort, thronged out, of course, to see the balloon; but it was with the greatest difficulty that anyone could be made to credit the actual voyage-the crossing of the Atlantic. The grapnel caught at 2 P.M. precisely; and thus the whole voyage was completed in 75 hours; or rather less, counting from shore to shore. No serious accident occurred. No real danger was at any time apprehended. The balloon was exhausted and secured without trouble; and when the MS. from which this narrative is compiled was dispatched from Charleston, the party were still at Fort Moultrie. Their further intentions were not ascertained; but we can safely promise our readers some additional information either on Monday or in the course of the next day, at furthest.

This is unquestionably the most stupendous, the most interesting, and the most important undertaking ever accomplished or even attempted by man. What magnificent events may ensue, it would be useless now to think of determining.

**THE END**

**Virginia Clemm Poe. Portrait painted after her death in January 1847.** ***Courtesy of the Library of Congress***

# Annabel Lee
# 1850

*Sartain's Union Magazine of Literature and Art*, January, 1850, Philadelphia. Original cover for the issue continuing the first publication of "Annabel Lee."
*Public Domain*

**"I remained too much inside my head and ended up losing my mind."**

**-- Edgar Allan Poe**

---

Virginia Clemm Poe was 24-years old when she died on January 30, 1847. During her five-year long illness Poe became increasingly despondent and started drinking heavily. After her death he refused to look at his wife's face, wanting to remember Virginia as a living – not dead – person. Ironically, the only surviving picture of Virginia was painted immediately after her death. (See page 132)

"Annabel Lee" was the last poem written by Poe before his mysterious death on October 7, 1849. The poem's meter and language are written in the style of an old English fairy tale. The opening phrase "It was many and many a year ago" is similar to "once upon a time."

Virginia is the obvious source as the inspiration of "Annabel Lee." But there is more at play emotionally than just the loss of a love. After Virginia's death, back in Richmond, Poe met his first youthful love, Elmira Royston Shelton, who was now a widow. Elmira and Poe rekindled their relationship after they discover that their letters to each other while he was in college had been intercepted by her parents. They became engaged and Poe left Richmond for a trip to Baltimore and New York, from which he never returned.

Poe's repeated use of the phrase "kingdom by the sea" is the most prominent clue to Charleston as the setting for this haunting poem. It is an obvious reference to Charleston's colonial prominence. The use of the term "maiden" is another clue, as Charleston was the most formal city in America, linking the city directly with the English tradition of gallant knights and maidens. There is also the local Charleston legend (discussed in the "Introduction") about the young Charleston maiden who died of unrequited love.

Written in the last months of his life, "Annabel Lee" is a fitting conclusion to his literary legacy. Following the death of Virginia, Poe was searching for an emotional anchor. In the poem Poe suggests that a powerful love can transcend death, a hope he surely held on the day he died in Baltimore.

"Annabel Lee" is a fitting end to one of the greatest literary figures in American history.

# ANNABEL LEE

---

It was many and many a year ago,
In a kingdom by the sea.
That a maiden there lived whom you might know
By the name of Annabel Lee;
And this maiden lived with no other thought
Than to love and be loved by me.

I was a child and she was a child
In this kingdom by the sea,
But we loved with a love that was more than love--
I and my Annabel Lee;
With a love that the winged seraphs of heaven
Coveted her and me.

And this was the reason that, long ago,
In this kingdom by the sea,
A wind blew out of a cloud, chilling
My beautiful Annabel Lee;
So that her high-born kinsmen came
And bore her away from me,
To shut her up in a sepulchre
In this kingdom by the sea.

The angels, not half so happy in heaven,
Went envying her and me--
Yes! that was the reason (as all men know,
In this kingdom by the sea)
That the wind came out of the cloud by night,
Chilling and killing my Annabel Lee.

But our love it was stronger by far than the love
Of those who were older than we--
Of many far wiser than we--
And neither the angels in Heaven above
Nor the demons down under the sea,
Can ever dissever my soul from the soul
Of the beautiful Annabel Lee.

For the moon never beams without bringing me dreams
Of the beautiful Annabel Lee;
And the stars never rise but I see the bright eyes
Of the beautiful Annabel Lee;
And so, all the night-tide, I lie down by the side
Of my darling--my darling--my life and my bride,
In her sepulchre there by the sea,
In her tomb by the sounding sea.

**Edgar Allan Poe, photo of painting by Mrs. Norman Burwell.**
***Courtesy of the Library of Congress***

# Bibliography

Ackroyd, Peter (2008). *Poe: A Life Cut Short*. London: Chatto & Windus.

Allen, Hervey. "Introduction". *The Works of Edgar Allan Poe*. New York: P. F. Collier & Son, 1927.

Bittner, William. *Poe: A Biography*. Boston: Little, Brown and Company, 1962.

Empric, Julienne H. "'A Note On Annabel Lee'", collected in *Poe Studies*. Volume VI, Number 1 (June 1973).

Hutchisson, James M. *Poe*. Jackson: University Press of Mississippi, 2005.

Kennedy, J. Gerald. *Poe, Death, and the Life of Writing*. New Haven: Yale University Press, 1987.

Krutch, Joseph Wood. *Edgar Allan Poe: A Study in Genius*. New York: Alfred A. Knopf, 1926.

Meyers, Jeffrey. *Edgar Allan Poe: His Life and Legacy*. Cooper Square Press, 1992. I

Quinn, Arthur Hobson. *Edgar Allan Poe: A Critical Biography*. Baltimore: The Johns Hopkins University Press, 1998.

Rosenheim, Shawn James. *The Cryptographic Imagination: Secret Writing from Edgar Poe to the Internet*. Baltimore: Johns Hopkins University Press, 1997.

Silverman, Kenneth. *Edgar A. Poe: Mournful and Never-ending Remembrance.* New York: Harper Perennial, 1991.

Sova, Dawn B. *Edgar Allan Poe: A to Z.* New York: Checkmark Books, 2001.

Stashower, Daniel. *The Beautiful Cigar Girl: Mary Rogers, Edgar Allan Poe, and the Invention of Murder.* New York: Dutton, 2006.

Thomas, Dwight & David K. Jackson. *The Poe Log: A Documentary Life of Edgar Allan Poe, 1809–1849.* Boston: G. K. Hall & Co., 1987.

Whalen, Terance. "Poe and the American Publishing Industry". In Kennedy, J. Gerald. *A Historical Guide to Edgar Allan Poe.* New York: Oxford University Press, 2001.

# About the Editor

Mark R. Jones is an author, historian and tour guide from Charleston, South Carolina. He is the author of five books about South Carolina history. He is also a popular lecturer on subjects such as murder, Prohibition, scandals, piracy, Jim Crow politics and jazz.

With his wife, Rebel Sinclair, Jones operates Black Cat Tours, named for their cats Edgar Allan Poe, Pluto, and Annabel Lee. Yes, they often tell Poe stories on their tours.

**BlackCatTours.com** **MarkJonesBooks.com**

# Also Available from East Atlantic Publishing

## From Rags to Ragtime – They Created the Soundtrack of the 20th Century!

For the first time here is the stirring story of the Jenkins Orphanage Band and its role in American popular music. From slavery to freedom, follow the inspirational rags-to-riches story of some of America's greatest jazz musicians all brought together by the determination of one man, a free black slave named Rev. Daniel Jenkins. His Jazz Nursery revolutionized the music world!

Illustrated with more than 70 photos.

History/Music/Culture: 9-780615-852034

Size: 6x9. 347 pp.

Available at your local bookstore, from Amazon or visit our web site: **EastAtlanticPublishing.com**

**843-647-7508**
editor@eastatlanticpublishing.com

Made in United States
North Haven, CT
16 March 2023